Heart of the Billionaire

THE BILLIONAIRE'S OBSESSION

Sam

J. S. SCOTT

Heart of the Billionaire

ISBN-10:1939962323
ISBN-13:978-1-939962-32-4

Acknowledgements

For all the wonderful readers who wanted to know what Sam did… you're about to find out.

To Mom and Dad for your love and support. Thanks for letting me read your romances when you had finished them, Mom. That got me started early on my addiction to romance novels.

Karma…as always….you amaze me with your friendship and support.

Many thanks to Cali MacKay from "Covers By Cali" for the awesome covers.

And to my husband for supporting my dreams.

~J.S.~

Contents

Prologue 1
Chapter 1 6
Chapter 2 16
Chapter 3 25
Chapter 4 36
Chapter 5 43
Chapter 6 55
Chapter 7 64
Chapter 8 75
Chapter 9 83
Chapter 10 93
Chapter 11 102
Chapter 12 113
Chapter 13 121
Chapter 14 134
Chapter 15 143
Epilogue 151

Prologue

September 15, 1996
HE sat next to me again today. I have to assume it's just a coinci-
dence, because I can't imagine why he would want to sit next to me
or give me one of his incredible smiles that appeared to light up the
rather dreary room of our college English Literature class. I'm not
sure if I'm happy or not about the fact that he sat right beside me.
Honestly, I had to look around to see exactly who he was smiling
at. Certainly not me. Not Madeline Reynolds, the plain redheaded
woman with the dorky glasses and too much meat on her bones.
But there was nobody else in the room at the time, so I suppose he
must have been smiling at me. I didn't smile back. And I had a very
hard time focusing on the classics with HIM sitting next to me.

September 16, 1996
HIS name is Sam Hudson. He introduced himself today. The man
makes my palms damp and my mouth go as dry as the desert
the moment I see him. When he reached out his hand today and
introduced himself, I had to wipe my hand on my jeans before I
stammered my name to him like a complete idiot. He was flashing

that smile at me again and I went completely brain dead, unable to find even one intelligent thing to say to him. Why does he have to be so handsome...and tall? Everything about the man is just... too much. Maybe tomorrow he'll sit next to someone else. I almost hope he does. He makes me too nervous. There's something strange about a handsome guy paying attention to me with so many other gorgeous women in the same classroom.

September 17, 1996
Sam caught up to me tonight after class to ask me if I wanted to study with him. He's doing the same thing that I am right now, working during the day and knocking out as many classes as he can toward a business degree in night courses. I have no doubt that he'll be successful in business. He has a hungry look, a determination to succeed in those beautiful emerald eyes of his. I told him I wanted to be a doctor. I'm not quite sure why I told him. I tell so few people because it's laughable that dirt-poor Maddie Reynolds, a girl shuffled from foster home to foster home, could actually aspire to be a doctor. Sam just smiled, but it wasn't a mocking one. Then he told me sincerely that he thought I'd make a great doctor. How could he know that? He doesn't even know me. But at least he wasn't laughing at me.

November 14, 1996
I've been so busy that I haven't had a chance to write for a while now. I'm doing all the double shifts at the nursing home that I possibly can, plus my classes. I have to have enough money to pay for my next semester. Sam took me to his apartment to study tonight, and he actually seemed embarrassed because it was a studio apartment that wasn't in the greatest neighborhood. I don't know why he should be embarrassed. He works so hard. His construction job is hard physical labor and I know that he usually works from early morning until evening nearly seven days a week. He's trying to get enough money to bring his mom and his younger brother here to Tampa to live. Sam talks mostly about the future,

probably because his past hasn't been so good. I can relate to that. I'd rather think about the future myself. I've only known Sam for a few months now, but he's become the best friend I've ever had except for Crystal, and she's been gone for so many years now. I feel a little silly that I ever had doubts about Sam. He's a very good person, the best man I've ever known. And he's so supportive about all of my goals. I just wish he'd get over calling me his "Sunshine" and pulling the rubber band out of my hair because he says it's a shame to confine such beautiful hair. Is the guy blind? My hair is absolutely tragic!

December 12, 1996
Sam said something to me today that I thought was strange. He said his friendship with me made him want to be a better man. I'm not sure what that was all about and he just shrugged casually when I asked him what he meant. How much better could he be? He works his ass off, tries to help his family, and is working to better himself by getting an education. Does he think being rich makes a man good? If so, I wish he wouldn't think that. Sam Hudson is fine just the way he is. He's perfect. I just wish he didn't have to work so hard.

January 10, 1997
Sam and I don't have any of the same classes this semester, but there is rarely a day that goes by that I don't speak to him. I don't know if I could stand not talking to him or seeing his handsome face. He makes me laugh when I'm tired and crabby, and I try to keep a tube of muscle relief cream around for when his body has been pushed to the limit from working so many hours. He tries to uplift my spirits while I try to relieve his physical pain. I guess that's what friendship is about. He stripped his t-shirt off today so I could put the cream on his back for him. Every time I do this, it gets more difficult to keep my hands from shaking, and I hate myself for it. Sam and I are friends. He gives me so much support and I've come to rely on his friendship. I'm a nursing assistant, for

God's sake. It isn't like I'm not familiar with the human body. It's just...Sam's body. His skin is always blazing hot and his muscles are tense. Sometimes he groans a deep, masculine groan of relief from his back pain when I apply the cream, and I flood between my thighs and my nipples get hard. I start thinking about other things than just his back pain. I know I shouldn't. But I do. I know most women have done "the deed" at my age, but I haven't. I've never wanted to. Not until I met Sam. But he's just a friend and I need to remind myself of that fact every single day, even though my heart and body want so much more.

February 14, 1997
It's Valentine's Day and something happened today, something extraordinary. Sam Hudson gave me a single red rose...and then he kissed me. It wasn't the usual peck on the cheek he gives me as a friend. It was a real, hot, wet, toe-curling kiss that made my heart pound and my body burn for more. We both came out of the kiss panting. I'm sure I looked dazed and confused because that's how I felt. Sam looked horrified. He cursed and started rambling about how he hadn't meant to do that and how I deserved so much better. He said I should have dozens of roses instead of just one. I told him that one red rose was so much better than anything anyone could ever do for me because it came from him. I cried. I couldn't help it. So he kissed me again...and again.

April 10, 1997
Sam and I have been a couple for two months now and he still won't do "the deed" with me. I want to. I've told him that. My body responds to his every touch, every kiss. I love him so much it hurts, but I haven't told him because he hasn't said it either and I'm not sure he wants to hear it. He says I purr like a kitten when he touches me, kisses me. Sadly, I think I do, but it's rather embarrassing. Not that I have a lot of experience, but I don't think any man can kiss like Sam. He knows that I'm a virgin. I told him. He says he's afraid to touch me sometimes because I'm too pure, too

good. If only he knew the dreams I have about him. He wouldn't think I was so very good at all. I love him so much and I want him to be my first. My only. I want to tell him that I love him, but I'm scared. What if he doesn't feel the same way?

May 12, 1997

I'm alone again, as I've always been. Sam and I were supposed to meet for coffee yesterday and as I approached the coffee shop, I saw them in the alleyway. The woman was beautiful—tall, thin, and pretty—everything I never have been and never will be. Sam's back was against the brick building and the woman was all over him, her hands in his hair, kissing my Sam like he belonged to her. His hands were on her breast and her butt, holding her model-thin body against his, grinding against her. I froze and stood there like a damn statue. I'm not sure how long I watched, my heart ready to pound out of my chest, unable to believe that it was really my Sam kissing that woman. But, oh my God, it was. When they came up for air, his eyes immediately met mine, the look on his face unmistakable. Guilt. Satisfaction. In that moment, my heart shattered into a million little pieces, and Sam knew it. He knew it and he didn't even try to explain. I doubt anything will ever put it back together again. I had to run away, and Sam just let me go without a single word. Was I really that stupid, that naïve? Did I really think that Sam Hudson was doing anything other than playing a game with me? Nobody has ever wanted me. Not as a child, nor as an adolescent. And not as an adult either. Most likely, no one ever will. I'll cry some more and then I'll sleep, and try to forget what it felt like to be wanted for a short time. It was all just a lie.

Chapter 1

D r. Madeline Reynolds chewed on her thumbnail, a look of total concentration on her face, as she flipped the pages of a medical file on one of her five-year-old patients at the clinic. It was seven p.m., way past time for her to get home and try to get some rest, but something about the case was nagging at her. She had to be missing something, something important. Timmy was tired, listless, having occasional vomiting and diarrhea, and it had to be more than a virus. The poor tyke had been that way for months.

Sighing, she leaned back in the chair of her office in the clinic, grimacing as she bit a little too hard on her fingernail. She'd need to consult a pediatrician, run more tests. Sending up a silent prayer that Timmy's mother would show up at her son's next appointment, Maddie closed the file. The poor kid didn't have an easy life, and his mother wasn't exactly consistent.

"Hello, Madeline."

A husky baritone sounded from the doorway of her office, causing her to leap to her feet, ready to push the alarm button on the side of her desk. The free clinic wasn't in a good neighborhood and poor Kara had already come close to getting shot there while she was volunteering.

"I didn't mean to scare you."

A cold chill ran down Maddie's spine, but not from fear. She recognized the voice. Eyes narrowing, she focused on the body and face behind that smooth-as-velvet masculine tone. "How did you get by Simon's security? And what in the hell are you doing here?"

Her friend Kara was engaged to be married to Sam's brother, Simon. Unfortunately, during the last year, that had forced her to be in close proximity to the man who had broken her heart so many years ago. Those meetings had been brief and incredibly tense. Luckily, she had managed to avoid any significant communication with him...until this moment.

Sam Hudson shrugged and stepped into the room as though he owned it. Even dressed casually in a pair of jeans and a burgundy cable-knit sweater, the man oozed power and arrogance, carried it on those wide shoulders like an elegant mantle. "They're my security, too, Sunshine. They work for Hudson. Do you think they would do anything other than let me by them with a polite good evening?"

Arrogant bastard. Maddie's heart raced and her palms grew moist. Simon and Sam were both billionaires, co-owners of Hudson Corporation. So, it was Sam's company, too, but she tried to ignore that fact as much as possible. She wiped her hands over her denim-clad thighs, wishing she hadn't showered and changed in the tiny shower in the back of the clinic before coming into her office. Maybe it would have been easier to face Sam in her professional attire, her hair confined in a conservative knot. Trying to push a flaming corkscrew spiral behind one ear, she stiffened her spine, trying to make herself appear taller than her five-foot-three height. "What do you want, Sam? This is hardly your neighborhood. And I don't think you need the services of a hooker?" Her voice was hard, brittle. Damn it. Why couldn't she act nonchalant? So many years had come and gone since that heart-shattering event with Sam. He was a stranger to her now. Why couldn't she treat him like one?

Moving closer, he answered darkly, "Would you care, Sunshine? Would it matter to you if I fucked every woman in the city?"

"Ha! Like you haven't already? And stop calling me by that ridiculous pet name." She answered sarcastically, but her heart was racing and her breath caught as he moved close enough for her to catch a whiff of his enticing smell of musk and man, a spicy aroma that made her slightly dizzy. His scent hadn't changed, and it was still as tempting as it had been all those years ago.

"Why are you still here? My security alerted me that you were here after dark. You should be home. This neighborhood isn't safe during the day, much less at night," he growled softly.

"Simon's security." Somehow, she couldn't associate the two men, even if they were brothers. Simon was nice and had a heart of gold underneath his gruff exterior. Sam was the devil himself, Satan disguised as a GQ model with more money and power than any man had the right to have. Especially a man like Samuel Hudson.

"What if some thug got through security, found you here alone and vulnerable?" He moved closer, so close she could feel his warm breath caressing her temple.

God, he was so tall, so broad and muscular. Sam had worked construction when she had known him years ago, hard physical labor that had given him a sculpted, perfect body. Strangely, it hadn't changed one single bit. How in the hell did a man maintain that awesome body sitting behind a desk? Backing away from his intimidating presence, her ass bumped against the desk, leaving her no space to move farther away.

"A man could take advantage of a woman alone in an empty office," he continued, his voice low, dangerous.

Maddie pushed against Sam's chest, trying to get free of her wedged-in position between him and the desk. "Move. Back off, Hudson, before I'm forced to send your balls into your throat."

His muscular thigh moved over hers, annihilating the possibility of being kneed in the groin. "I taught you that move, remember? And never tell your attacker your intentions, Madeline."

She craned her neck and looked at him, his emerald green eyes watching her carefully. Just as it had years ago, his handsome face took her breath away. He'd always reminded her of some ancient

Instructions for making a bar graph:

- Study one set of information. Figure out the title for your horizontal axis ("game number") and plot the game numbers on your graph.
- Study the other set of information. Figure out the title for your vertical axis ("number of goals scored") and plot the numbers on your graph.
- Record the information at the proper points on your graph as you did on the line graph. However, instead of connecting the points with a line, fill in the column under each point to form a bar.

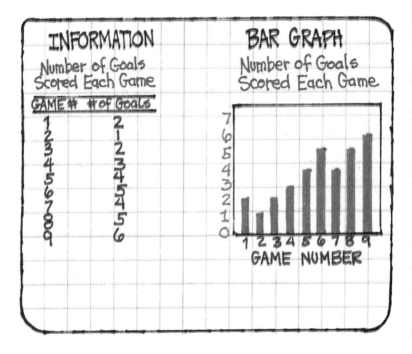

Instructions for making a pictograph:
- Choose which set of information you want to illustrate with symbols (number of goals scored).
- Select a symbol and decide on its value. Record the symbol and the value in the key. For example, you might use one soccer ball to stand for one goal.
- Study the other set of information. Figure out the titles for your vertical axis and plot them on your graph (list of games by number).
- Record the information by drawing the proper number of symbols in each row.

Instructions for making a circle graph:

A circle graph is a little more difficult to make. It takes some extra supplies as well as some extra figuring. You will need

- a percentage protractor (it's much easier to use than a regular protractor),
- a compass,
- paper,
- a ruler, and
- a pencil.

Start as you would with the other graphs.

- Begin with the title. Ask yourself, "What major question will my circle graph answer?" For example, you might want to find out how you spend your time. Your title might be "My 24-Hour Day."
- Gather the information and divide it into segments.
- Assign each segment a value.
- Change the value into a percentage.

MY 24-HOUR DAY

Segment Title	Value (in hours)	Value (in percentages)
Body Maintenance *	12 HRS.	50%
School	6 HRS.	25%
Chores Homework	3 HRS	12 ½%
Free time	3 HRS	12 ½%
* Eating Sleeping Exercising		

WHAT A LIFE!

Now it's time to draw your circle graph.

- Draw a circle with the compass. Make sure it is large enough to hold all your segment titles.
- Place the percentage protractor over the circle and mark the percentages for each segment.
- Using the ruler, draw the lines for the segments according to your marks.
- Label each segment with the proper title and value.

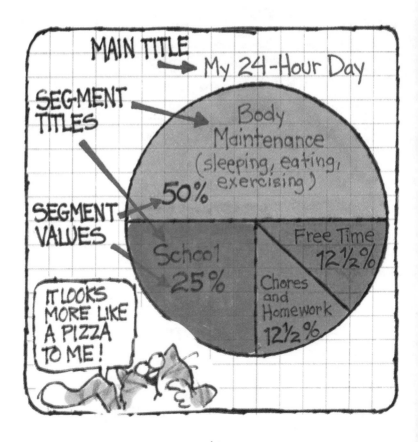

WARNING!

If you try the ideas in this book, you will be able to *read* and *make* charts and graphs...

...you might even have fun doing it!

THE END

About the Author

Marilyn Berry has a master's degree in education with a specialization in reading. She is on staff as a creator of supplementary materials at Living Skills Press. Marilyn and her husband Steve Patterson have two sons, John and Brent.

blond god, so damn perfect that his body and features should be carved in marble. However, at the moment, he might be as *hard* as marble, but he was far from cold. Heat emanated from his body in waves, his eyes just as fiery and molten. "Go fuck yourself, Hudson."

Sam's lips turned up, twitching precariously like he was trying not to grin. His hands splayed over her back, pulling her body completely into his as he whispered into her ear, "I'd rather fuck you, Sunshine. Much more satisfying. You're still the most beautiful woman I've ever seen. Even more beautiful than you were years ago."

Liar. He's such a damn liar. If I had been so desirable he wouldn't have done what he did. "Let go and get the hell out of my office." The bastard was playing her, and it was intolerable. She wasn't beautiful and she was nothing like the twiggy blonde models who he sported on his arm and took to his bed.

"Kiss me first. Prove to me that there isn't something left unfinished between us," Sam answered, his dark green eyes lit with sparks of fire, his voice hard and demanding.

"The only thing left unfinished is the fact that you never even said you were sorry for what you did. You didn't give a damn. You didn't—"

Maddie never got a chance to finish. Sam's hot, hard mouth smothered her bitter words, never asking, simply demanding her response. His large, agile hands moved down her back, grasping her ass and lifting her to a sitting position on the desk, making it easier for him to devour her mouth.

Sam never just kissed: he branded, he claimed. Maddie moaned into his mouth as his tongue thrust and retreated, thrust and retreated, until she was breathless. Surrendering, her arms wound around his neck, her hands fisting his silken wavy locks of hair, savoring the fall of softness over her fingertips.

Wrapping her legs around his hips, needing to somehow find an anchor to keep her from drifting away in a tidal wave of lust, she allowed her tongue to duel with his, feeling his arousal against her heated core. Her hips surged against his erection with every hard thrust of his tongue.

Sam groaned, his hands delving under her sweatshirt, his fingertips stroking over the bare skin of her back, making her shiver with longing.

Maddie was drowning, lost in a sea of desire and need, slowly being pulled under the surface by a force stronger than her will.

I have to stop. This has to end before I'm completely lost.

Yanking her head back, her mouth disconnected from Sam's, leaving her panting for oxygen and completely shaken. Sam pulled her head forward to rest against his heaving chest.

"Shit. Maddie. Maddie," he choked out, one hand spearing into her curls, stroking her hair reverently.

Oh, God. No. She couldn't be sucked in by Sam Hudson again. Not in any way. She shoved hard against his chest, twisting away and lowering her legs until her feet hit the floor. "Get off me."

Fury built to a raging inferno inside her. How dare he use her, play with her because he was bored and she was the only available female in the building? Sam Hudson was a playboy, a man who took women to his bed and discarded them, finding another plaything soon after he was done with the last one. He was rarely seen with the same woman more than once. Did the man have a conscience? Did he care about no one but himself?

Maddie wanted to curl up into a little ball to protect herself, shamed by the way she had responded to Sam even though he was a complete dog. What kind of a person did that make her?

She shrugged away from him, turning her back to sprint for the door.

"Maddie. Wait." Sam's voice was husky, pleading yet demanding.

He grasped her arm, swinging her to face him before she was able to get to the door. Maddie turned to face him, her fury and fear battling for dominance. "Don't touch me again. Ever. I'm not the stupid, naïve woman you once knew. I trusted you once, and I forgave myself because I was young. I won't do it again. I don't have the excuse of youth to even justify being that stupid."

"You still want me," Sam answered vehemently, his eyes raking over her body, settling on her face.

Looking him straight in the eye, she answered angrily, "No, I don't. My body might respond to a gorgeous man, but it's just physiological, a sexual reaction. You," she poked a hand to his chest as she spat out, "mean absolutely nothing to me anymore."

"You want me to fuck you until you scream. I can still make you purr, Kitten," he told her arrogantly, a satisfied smirk on his face.

She shrugged, trying to force down her violent desire to slap the conceited look from his handsome face. "I wouldn't know. You've never fucked me. And you never will."

Wrenching her arm from his hold, Maddie stormed through the office door, scooping her jacket from the hook by the reception desk and bolting through the lobby and out the front door of the clinic. She didn't look back. She couldn't. One of Hudson's security officers escorted her to her car and she drove away as if she were a convicted criminal with the law on her tail, wanting nothing more than to get as far away from Sam as she could possibly get.

Maddie drove in a daze, two words playing through her hazy brain like a broken record.

Never again.

Never again.

Sam Hudson walked slowly through the reception area of the clinic, lost in his own thoughts. What the hell had just happened? He'd stopped to see if Maddie was okay, concerned that she was still at the clinic so late—a quick stop to make sure all was well because he knew she was here alone. Damn. Could he ever see the woman and not want to possess her, make her want him as much as he wanted her?

You've never gotten over her. You probably never will. She's haunted you for years. She got under your skin like a sliver of wood that's always a little bit raw and irritated, never working its way out again.

Stepping outside, Sam closed the door behind him. He glanced at one of his security officers. "Can you lock up?"

The man nodded. "Yes, sir. Hope your meeting with Dr. Reynolds went okay."

Sam barked a humorless, self-mocking laugh. "Yeah. It was very informative." *I learned that she still fucking hates me as much as she ever did.* He lifted a hand to the other guards as he departed, making his way to his vehicle.

Yep. That meeting had gone really well, he thought darkly as he stepped into his Bugatti and started the engine.

You never even said you were sorry.

Her words haunted him, would probably always haunt him now. "Fuck!" Sam slammed his fist against the steering wheel in frustration. Nope. He hadn't ever said he was sorry. Then again, he hadn't been able to say it back then. Still, he should have said it, found a way to apologize later. It hadn't been possible after the incident had taken place, and he had just blown his second chance a few minutes ago.

What was it about Maddie that made him lose his reason?

You're acting like an asshole because she doesn't really care about you anymore and it's eating you alive. You might be able to have her body if you seduce her…but never her heart. Never again.

Once, years ago, Maddie had looked at him with eyes that sparkled with admiration, adoration. One brief incident and he had washed that look from her beautiful eyes forever.

Leaning his forehead against the steering wheel, he closed his eyes, still able to picture the Maddie who had looked at him with respect and affection even when he hadn't had two pennies to rub together. It was ironic: now that he was one of the wealthiest men in the world, she eyed him like a bug that needed to be squashed, a rodent that needed to be exterminated.

You'll see her again. She'll be forced to talk to you for Simon and Kara's wedding. The wedding was being held in his home, so Maddie wouldn't have a choice. He was the best man and she was the maid of honor. Maddie would have to at least be civil, and Sam knew she would. She was considerate and loyal to anyone she considered a friend. Her own feelings would take a back seat to making sure Kara had a happy wedding, one with no hassles or ugliness.

And no matter how Maddie treats me, no matter how she looks at me, I won't be a dick to her. Shit. I hope she doesn't bring a guy with her. I never asked Simon if she was involved with anyone.

Sam sat back in his seat with a heavy sigh and put his car in gear, wondering if it was even possible anymore for him *not* to be an asshole. Truth was, the years had changed him, made him into a man who he wasn't at all certain he liked anymore. And if Maddie had a man in her life, he was even more likely to lose it.

Find a woman, someone to take your mind off Maddie.

Snapping his seatbelt on as he backed out of the parking space, Sam took a deep breath and ran through a mental list of possible willing females…until he caught a tantalizing smell, an elusive scent that clung tenaciously to his sweater. Her fragrance. A reminder of what had just occurred in her office.

"Fuck! I can't do it. I can't be with another woman. Not now," he whispered to himself, pissed off that he had kissed her, that he had felt her lush curves against his body. Now, the thought of spending the night in the bed of any other woman but Maddie left him cold. Honestly, it had left him cold since the moment he had seen Madeline again over a year ago.

Sam braked his vehicle at the exit of the parking lot, glancing quickly at his watch, grinning as he turned left instead of right, headed toward Simon's condo.

It was time.

Simon had called him earlier, informing Sam that he was going to be an uncle, and asking for a favor, which was a complete rarity for Simon. There was nothing Sam wouldn't do for his little brother. He had failed to protect Simon once, and it wasn't happening ever again. Whatever Simon needed, he'd be there for him.

Thank God Simon had found Kara. Sam adored his brother's fiancée, wanting to kiss the ground she walked on, simply because she loved his little brother unconditionally, made Simon happier than Sam had ever seen him. And Simon deserved that happiness, that kind of devotion from a woman. Unfortunately, watching Simon and Kara together made Sam realize just how empty his own life was, how desolate and superficial his existence had become.

Like I haven't always known that? Nothing has been real since I lost Maddie.

Kissing Maddie, holding her again after all those years, had made things even worse. It was like something was awakening deep inside him, a sensation that was familiar, yet not. Certainly, it wasn't comfortable.

Forget her. Forget what it felt like to lose yourself in Maddie's softness, her scent, the feel of her lush curves and deliciously eager mouth.

Sam cursed, knowing he'd be sleeping alone tonight, taking himself in hand as he fantasized about Maddie. And this time, those memories would be much more vivid, newer, more real than ever before.

Fuck! He was so completely screwed…and definitely not in a good way.

Maddie turned the page of the book on her lap, wondering why she just didn't give up and go to bed. It wasn't like she was really absorbing any of the written words.

"Damn it," she whispered, slamming the book closed and dropping it on the table beside the sofa. Honestly, she didn't want to go to bed. If she did, she would just keep remembering her encounter with Sam, torturing herself with memories of that scorching hot kiss earlier in the evening.

Swiping the remote control from the table, she pushed the button to activate the television, hoping she could drown out her thoughts with the ten o'clock news.

Her doorbell rang just as the news anchor started recounting the top stories of the day.

Who the hell could it be? She had no family and none of her friends would come to her door at this time of night unless it was an emergency. She sprang to her feet and sprinted to the door, her heart racing. Looking through the peephole, she saw a man in uniform, a Hudson security uniform.

"Who is it and what do you want?" she called loudly through the door.

"Special Valentine's Day delivery for Dr. Reynolds," the man called back.

"Leave it and go." There was no way she was opening her door, even if the guy was apparently from Hudson.

"I understand, ma'am. I'll just leave it here on the doorstep." He bent, and then straightened again and left.

Maddie opened the door a crack, leaving the security chain in place. She watched the man get into his truck and drive away. She lifted the chain and opened the door completely, her eyes widening.

On her doorstep was the most incredible bouquet of red roses she had ever seen. There were several dozen flowers, too many for her to count in her stunned condition. Lifting the heavy, sturdy vase that appeared to be made of crystal, she secured the door behind her and lugged the roses to her dining room table. Placing them in the middle of the circular oak surface, she plucked the card from the center of the arrangement.

She sat, her shaky knees barely able to support her legs. The card was small, the outside of the tiny envelope decorated with hearts and a cute little Cupid in the corner. The only thing on the front was her name. She opened it with trembling fingers, yanking the notecard from its surrounding paper. There, in handwriting she still recognized, were only two words.

I'm sorry.

There was no signature, no other identifying markings.

Dropping both the envelope and card on the table, Maddie buried her face in her hands and wept.

Chapter 2

*E*nough! This is complete bullshit.

Sam Hudson shoved his cell phone into the pocket of his gray Armani suit and hit the brakes of his Bugatti, jamming the pedal so hard that the tires squealed in protest, before shifting gears and doing a completely illegal U-turn in the middle of a Tampa side street. Gritting his teeth, he hit the gas and flew in the opposite direction, away from his waterfront mansion home.

What in hell is she doing? Trying to kill herself?

Honestly, Dr. Maddie Reynolds was about to kill *him.* She was in her Tampa free clinic again. After dark. In a crappy area of Tampa. She'd been there every evening now for two weeks, his security alerting him every time she was there at night. For fourteen goddamn days he'd waited at home to hear from his security that she had safely left the area for the night. Every night it was after eleven. Tonight was day fifteen and it was midnight. And Maddie still hadn't left the clinic.

She was seeing patients, on a volunteer basis, every night at the clinic after she finished in her regular job as a hospitalist. Obviously, she stayed later doing the necessary paperwork and case evaluations after she closed the clinic around nine o'clock, sometimes ten. When she had blocks of days off, she spent them there in the clinic. All day. And half the damn night. There was no way she could keep up this kind of schedule and not drop from exhaustion.

Slamming his palm against the steering wheel in frustration, Sam was determined to find out what the hell was going on. Maddie had always worked like a fiend, doing tons of hours for no pay at her free clinic on her off days, but not like this, not every single night. She had security from Hudson there because his brother Simon had arranged it after his fiancée, Kara, had nearly been shot during a robbery at the facility, but it still wasn't safe, and Maddie's hours were ridiculous. Did she ever sleep? Did she eat?

Sam hadn't seen Maddie since his encounter with her at the clinic nearly a month ago, a brief interlude that he was having a difficult time forgetting. All he had to do was think about that kiss, or smell her scent on the sweater he had been wearing that night—a garment that, for some strange reason, he hadn't yet thrown into his pile for dry cleaning—and his cock was hard enough to pound nails.

Shit. She's making me insane.

Scowling, he cut a hard right turn and accelerated, his heart thumping at the thought of seeing Maddie again, wondering what she had made of the flowers he had sent her on Valentine's Day. Once, years ago, he'd only been able to afford to give her a single red rose. Now, he had finally given her the dozens of roses she deserved. Yeah, it was a shitty way to apologize for what had happened all those years ago, but he'd never been especially good with apologies. He was Sam Hudson, billionaire and co-owner of the Hudson Corporation. Hell, he hadn't apologized for anything since…well…ever, except for his drunken actions at Simon's birthday party the year before. Okay, he had probably apologized years ago, but not since his mother had grabbed his ear when he was a kid and made him answerable for his bad behavior. He'd made a habit of not doing anything he might end up regretting, excluding that incident with Maddie so many years ago and the more recent incident with Kara. Even now, he couldn't actually be completely regretful for what he had done to Maddie, except for the part where he had hurt her with his actions. Really, his only apology in years had been the one to Kara and his brother for his behavior at Simon's birthday party. He had been drunk, depressed. But it still didn't excuse his shitty behavior. Luckily, Simon and Kara had forgiven him, leaving the incident in the past.

I hurt Maddie, the one person who I never wanted to hurt.

But he had, and for that, he *was* sorry.

She'll never forgive me.

Sam's jaw clenched as he turned left, getting closer to the clinic, into a seedier area of the city. Yeah, he knew that Maddie was lost to him, had known it since the moment he had alienated her forever. Pain still ripped through his chest when he thought about the shattered look on Maddie's face, the devastation in her beautiful, hazel eyes. That was the day he had lost his Sunshine, and even after his years of success, the money, the power—his life was still fucking overcast, and sometimes downright gloomy.

I can still be her friend even though she hates me. I owe that to her as a friend. She's killing herself with work and I have to stop her.

"Shit," Sam cursed in a low, fervent voice. Who was he trying to fool? He wasn't an altruistic type of guy. Truth was, he wanted to see her, wanted to protect her. The rehearsal dinner for Simon and Kara's wedding was tomorrow and Maddie would be there, but he couldn't take another night of worrying about her. He was ending this now, before the crazy female made herself sick from pulling too many hours without enough sleep.

He didn't bother to pull into the parking lot. He steered his expensive sports car up to the curb and exited, waving to the two Hudson guards in front of the clinic.

"She still here?" he asked one of the guards closest to the door.

"Yes, sir. Hasn't left yet." The older man quickly brought forward a key to unlock the door.

She will. Right fucking now.

Sam pushed open the door, his irritation making his stomach churn. As he strode through the lobby, he heard the loud click of the door being locked behind him. Ignoring it, he strode through the reception area and into the back offices. He stopped, taking a deep breath before he opened the door of Maddie's office, preparing himself for an ugly confrontation.

His pent-up breath exited his body in an audible *whoosh* as he realized there would be no warfare in the immediate future. His intended opponent, dressed in an old pair of green scrubs, her fiery curls spread out over the desk and her right arm bent and supporting her head…was fast asleep.

Making his way to her desk, he scowled as he noticed the dark circles under her eyes. Still, the woman looked like an angel, her unblemished skin a creamy ivory, her mouth the color of ripe straw berries. Scanning her face, he realized she wasn't even wearing make-up, probably having showered after her clinic hours. He brought his hand gently to the back of her head, her damp hair confirming his suspicions about the shower. Giving in to the urges he was trying to hold in check, he buried his hand in her abundant curls, letting her fiery hair spill over his fingers.

"Shit," he muttered softly, fingering the tresses gently, indulging himself as her light floral scent wafted over his senses. He crouched, bringing his face level with hers. "Maddie," he called gently, his hand still caressing her hair.

She lifted her left hand, which had been resting on her thigh, and swatted at him, missing as he lurched backward to avoid the feeble swing. "Need to rest my eyes for a minute. Just a minute," she mumbled, her lips turning down into a frown, as though irritated.

Sam's lips curled up in an amused smile as he rubbed her scalp. "Time to sleep, Sunshine."

Maddie slapped at him again, this time hitting his shoulder in a pathetic, half-hearted smack. "Sleeping. Go away," she muttered, her eyes remaining closed.

Christ. She's really out of it.

Placing his hand against her mug of coffee, he noticed it was barely warm. She hadn't been out for long, but obviously she was exhausted, so sleep-deprived that her cognitive function was incredibly slow.

Sam slid her weekly planner out from under her arm, glancing quickly at the open page. Hmmm. She was off work for the next five days. Not that he was really surprised. All of the functions for Simon and Kara's wedding were starting tomorrow, beginning with the rehearsal and the rehearsal dinner.

Snapping the planner closed, he slid it into the pocket of his suit and rolled her chair back, her delectable ass still planted in it, just enough to slide one arm under her knees and the other behind her back. "Time for bed, Maddie," he whispered in a husky voice.

"Tired," she said, irritated. "Go away."

Sam glanced at Maddie's face as he stood with the petite bundle of femininity in his arms. She hadn't even opened her eyes. But she was still feisty. Head resting against his shoulder, she stirred, her arms creeping around his neck instinctively to make herself more comfortable. "Can't carry me. I'm too fat," she protested, her words slurred as if drunk.

Maddie's comment was so ridiculous that Sam grinned at her, raking his eyes over her body as he shifted her weight against his chest. She had a body made for sin, a body that had always been the most unholy temptation he had ever seen. Sam liked a woman with curves, and Maddie had them in abundance. Her breasts would fill a man's hands, and her skin was like silk. That ample, curvaceous ass was firm, and he got hot just fantasizing about those shapely thighs wrapped around his waist, Maddie urging him to fuck her. Just the feel of her softness against him made his cock strain against the zipper of his pants, eager to bury itself inside her, lose himself in that petite, curvy body.

Maddie never did like her body even though she's my ideal.

He chuckled as he snagged her purse from the back of the office chair, placing it on her abdomen as he strolled out of the office and to the lobby. Stopping at the locked door, he waited for security to open the outer door, putting his mouth to Maddie's ear. "You have the body of a goddess, Sunshine," he told her in a low, graveled voice, knowing she wasn't coherent, but needing to tell her regardless.

"Too fat," she answered on a soft sigh.

"Perfect," he answered, amused.

"Ugly red hair," she whispered, her eyes still closed.

"Beautiful," he retorted.

"You're crazy," she said with a feminine grunt of irritation.

"Probably," he admitted, exiting through the door as his employee opened it and stopping at the passenger side of his Bugatti. The guard caught Sam's subtle message and rushed to open the door of the automobile.

Maddie let loose another soft sigh, her warm breath caressing his neck. Sam bit back a groan.

Breathing a sigh of relief, Sam deposited Maddie's cuddly body into the seat. He couldn't be that close to her. Her scent, the feel of her body made him fucking insane. He fastened her seatbelt and settled her handbag into her lap before closing the door. Taking a deep breath, he moved around the car, lifting his hand in a silent gesture of thanks to his helpful security employee as he opened the driver's door and settled himself into his seat. Closing the door, he started the engine and strapped on his own seatbelt, his gaze drifting back to Maddie.

Shit! He hated seeing Maddie this way, so obviously exhausted. Even if it rankled, he'd rather see her spitting fire at him, her eyes flashing, her voice dripping with sarcasm or anger. Seeing her look so tired, so lost, so vulnerable ripped his fucking heart from his chest.

Tearing his eyes away from her, he shifted his Veyron into gear, making a decision that was definitely going to piss her off, but deciding he didn't give a shit. No doubt, if he didn't intervene, she'd be right back in action in the morning, hauling her drained body out of bed and into the clinic before the rehearsal and dinner the following afternoon.

Not happening! So what if she hates me for it? She already knows that I'm an asshole. Doesn't matter. As long as she's healthy.

He plugged his cell phone into its dashboard holder, intending to make some calls as he swung the car into a U-turn and headed back in the same direction he had been driving earlier.

He grinned, shooting a quick glance at Maddie before he dialed the first number, barking orders into the phone even though it was after one o'clock in the morning. Luckily, his personal assistant was sharp, and responded immediately. It wasn't every night that Sam called him at this hour; in fact, Sam never had called his PA at this hour, and David caught on instantly that the orders were important to his boss.

Totally oblivious, Maddie slumbered on, unaware of the fact that she was about to take a short vacation, whether she wanted it or not.

Sam deposited Maddie onto his ridiculously high-thread count Egyptian cotton sheets and watched as she snuggled into the soft fabric, tugging the pillow under her head with a satisfied moan—a throaty, erotic sound that nearly had him panting.

There's never been a day when I haven't panted after her, not since the first time I laid eyes on her.

Yeah, he'd wanted her then, too. His eyes had zoomed in on that bright, fiery mane of hers, pulled back from her face and cascading down her back, his cock jerking as his eyes landed on her beautiful face with those oh-so-conservative glasses perched on her nose, a slight frown of confusion on her cherry-red lips. She'd looked like a damn naughty librarian, and he'd gotten instantly hard every time he'd seen her from that day forward.

Wonder what happened to her glasses?

Gently, Sam lifted one of her eyelids to make sure she wasn't wearing contacts that needed to be removed, chuckling as she grunted with displeasure at the invasion. Satisfied that she must have had her vision corrected with laser surgery, he pulled his hand away from her face and sighed. Damn…he used to love to pull those glasses from her face and kiss her breathless. A small part of him mourned the loss, but a larger portion was relieved that she could see and that she had been able to get rid of the hated glasses.

He pulled off her tennis shoes and let them drop to the floor, deciding she could sleep in her scrubs. They were obviously clean and probably comfortable.

He stripped, watching her sleep while he discarded his clothing, disrobing until he stood only in his boxer briefs. Walking around the bed, he slipped between the sheets on the other side, flipping off the light beside his bed, his body tense. It was a big bed, but it wasn't big enough. Was he completely insane? How the fuck was he supposed to sleep with Maddie in his bed? This moment was surreal, an event he had dreamed about forever and fantasized about often.

Go to sleep, asshole. You're watching over her. If you don't stay with her, she'll probably sneak out before you can catch her.

Oh, hell no. There was no way she was working tomorrow. *That* bullshit needed to stop.

Punching his pillow, he rolled to his side, facing Maddie. God, she was beautiful. Everything about her was absolutely perfect. Unable to stop himself, he reached out his hand, scooting closer to her, as though drawn by a magnet. He fingered her curls, and then ran the back of his hand down her delicate face. The room was lit only by moonlight, but it was bright enough to see her features. As he ran his hand down her arm, she stirred, her eyelids fluttering. Her body moving restlessly, she inched toward him until she was rubbing against him, her body plastered against his entire front. Her arms circled his neck, nestling against his body like she belonged there.

"She does," he whispered fiercely. "There's no way she could feel this fucking good unless she belongs here with me."

"Sam?" she murmured in a confused voice.

His heart thundering, he answered, "Yeah?"

"I hate you. Why are you here?" She snuggled against him, belying her words as she clung to his fiery body like a heat-seeking missile.

"I know you do, Sunshine. Just sleep," he answered gravely.

He wrapped his arms around her. She might hate him, but she needed him right now. And he was determined to be there for her.

Like I should have been all along. I didn't fucking know she had never gotten married. Unless she got married and didn't change her name. But what sort of guy would let his woman work the way she does? I thought she'd have half a dozen kids by now.

Sam figured she must at least have a man in her life and he shuddered at the thought.

Mine. She fucking belongs here with me.

Closing his eyes, he let his senses absorb her fragrance, the feel of her body pressed against him.

It was agony and ecstasy all at once.

He lay there, listening to Maddie's steady, even breathing, indicating that she'd finally settled and was deeply asleep.

Strangely enough, Sam followed her into slumber moments later, his body relaxing, and his mind, for the first time in years, completely content.

Chapter 3

Maddie woke the next morning confused, her head pounding like she had the mother of all hangovers—except for the fact that she rarely drank more than a glass of wine. *What in the hell happened? Where am I?*

Pushing the hair back from her face, she blinked as she opened her eyes, her whole head foggy.

Hearing a masculine groan beneath her, she pushed to sit up, her fingers greeted by hot skin and tight muscle as she pushed against an enormous male chest.

What the hell?!

Maddie's eyes grew wide, coming totally awake in seconds as she looked at the body beneath hers. "Hudson," she hissed, noticing that she was straddling him, torso to torso, her head having previously rested on his shoulder. "Take your hands off my ass."

His eyes were wide open, shooting her a hot, intense look that nearly incinerated her. Her heart thundered as his sizzling green eyes devoured her.

"You called me Sam last night, Sunshine," he told her in a low, sultry voice. "And if you're going to spread that luscious body out on top of me, you should expect to have this delicious ass groped. I'm not exactly a saint."

Maddie shivered as he cupped her ass in his hands, bringing her core flush with his raging erection. *Last night? Last night? What exactly had happened?* Thinking furiously, she tried to remember if she and Sam had been…intimate. The last thing she remembered was putting her head on her desk at the clinic, just thinking she needed to rest her burning eyes for a moment. And then…nothing. "I can't remember last night. Did we—" She stopped abruptly, unable to ask Sam Hudson *that* mortifying question.

"Did we fuck?" he asked her casually. He released a beleaguered masculine sigh as he continued, "Sadly…no, we didn't. But if we had, you would have remembered it."

Thank God!

Swinging her leg over his body, she scrambled away from him, moving to the other side of the bed. Swiping the irritating curls from her face, she gave him an annoyed glance. She was still dressed in the clean scrubs she had donned after her shower at the clinic. He, however, was naked—at least from the waist up. She tried not to notice that sculpted chest, covered in a light dusting of blond hair, and the enticing trail that went down his navel to his…

Shit!

Pulling her eyes away from him, completely disgusted with herself for drooling over his ripped body, she asked abruptly, "What happened? Why am I here?" She assumed that this was his home, since she was in the same bed as him. A bed, that she had to admit, had damn nice sheets, in a bedroom with lovely furnishings.

Sam sat up, and Maddie held her breath as the sheet slipped lower, her eyes drawn unerringly back to his abdomen. Then, she noticed the elastic band that sat low on his hips, proof that he wasn't completely naked. She released her breath, hating herself for being disappointed.

"I'd love to tell you that I came to your clinic and you were so overcome with lust that you begged me to take you home and fuck you," he replied, his hot green eyes raking her face and body. "But you weren't and I didn't. I went to your office and you were fast asleep on your desk. I tried to wake you but you were so exhausted that I had to carry you here and put you to bed."

Sliding from the bed, she asked, "Why? I would have woken up eventually." She put her hands on her hips, annoyed that he had invaded her clinic. Again.

Flipping back the covers, he stood, shooting her a dangerous look. "Are you fucking kidding me? You were out for the count. What in the hell are you trying to do, Maddie? Kill yourself with exhaustion? Nobody crashes that hard unless they've been drinking or are entirely sleep-deprived. It's bullshit," he growled, walking across the room to retrieve a gray silk robe from a chair.

She opened her mouth to give him a scathing reply, but closed it as she watched him swagger across the room. Holy glutes, the man had an ass so tight that she could see every movement, every muscle contract and release as he strode across the room. Now *that* was the kind of ass a *woman* wanted to grope. Sam was ripped *everywhere*. He was damn near perfect, so incredibly masculine that he took her breath away. He still had the light scars on his back, strips of lighter skin that she had asked him about years ago but had never gotten a clear answer as to how he had gotten them.

Shrugging into the robe, he turned, giving her a quick glimpse of his morning erection that was prominently outlined by the snug undergarments. Catching her eyes with his, he smirked and raised a naughty brow.

Don't look at him. This is Sam Hudson. Asshole extraordinaire. He might look incredible, but his heart is as black as coal.

Jerking her eyes away from that teasing emerald glance, she tried to remember what she wanted to say. *Oh, yeah.* "What I do is none of your business. You had no right to abduct me from my office."

He snorted. "You weren't exactly complaining. You had your arms around my neck when I carried you to the car."

Oh, shit. "You carried me?"

He held his hand up in warning. "Don't go there. Your body is perfect." His face was fierce as he continued. "What have you been doing at the clinic at all hours? You already have a full-time job. You can't keep carrying both loads."

"I have to. Those people need me," she whispered. "They don't have anyone else to go to."

Maddie had left her private practice almost a year ago to work as a hospitalist, hoping she could spend more time at the clinic. She had more days off to spend at the clinic, but it did make for a heavy workload and she was feeling the strain.

Sam's face softened as he approached her. "You can't save the world, Maddie. You're only one person. It won't bring Crystal back."

Maddie flinched, the mention of her childhood best friend still causing her pain. Crystal had died at the age of ten from bacterial meningitis because she hadn't gotten treatment soon enough, her poverty-stricken parents having no insurance. *I must have told Sam years ago and he still remembers it.* It was one of the reasons she had wanted to be a doctor, and was still her primary motivation to keep the clinic open.

She looked up at him, leaning back against the thick bedpost. "Don't you think I know that? I had a five-year-old kid who I almost didn't diagnose in time. He was chronically sick, tired, fatigued. It took a while to do the testing because I'm not at the clinic every day. He had Type 1 diabetes. He could have died." She dropped her head, staring at the carpet, thinking of what could have happened had she not finally found a correct diagnosis. "I have to spend as much time there as I can." The incident with Timmy had scared her, made her push herself harder. What if there was another case out there, one who she couldn't get to in time?

Sam crowded her, pressing his large bulk against her, wedging her between his powerful body and the post. Taking her chin between his fingers, he tipped her head up, her gaze meeting his intense, penetrating look. "He didn't die, because you were there. But you aren't helping the working poor by exhausting yourself. There's a limit to what you can do."

"I need—"

"You need rest. You need to be able to fully function to give the best care you can," he told her sternly. "I know you, Maddie. You were a crusader even when we were younger. You can't save the world. You have to help one person at a time and hope you can make a difference." He yanked her into his arms, pressing her head against his chest as he stroked her hair. "I always knew you'd be a phenomenal doctor, but it will eat your soul if you let it. You take the responsibility of the world on your shoulders. You always have."

Maddie sighed, giving herself one moment to relax against the strong male body holding her, making her feel so safe, forgetting for just a brief time that she hated Sam Hudson. "I don't know what to do," she admitted. And it was true. She was so torn between her need to survive, pay her bills every month, and her desperation to help the people who truly needed medical care but couldn't afford it.

"I have a proposition for you," Sam answered, his hand moving soothingly up and down her back.

"What?" Pushing on his chest, she glanced up at him curiously.

"We can talk about it at breakfast. I'm starving," he answered casually.

"No. I need to shower and get to the clinic. Shit! I don't have any clothes here. I'll have to wear the same scrubs and—"

"You'll find everything you need in the master bath. I had my personal assistant pick up some things for you." He moved back and motioned toward a door on the other side of the bedroom. "I'll use the other bathroom and meet you in the kitchen."

"I told you I have to go. I have appointments today," she answered stubbornly, walking across the bedroom toward the bathroom.

"Actually, you don't," he answered as he yanked clothing from his closet.

"I have a full schedule until the wedding rehearsal," she informed him indignantly. Really, did he think she was so out of it that she had forgotten her appointments?

"You don't. Your clinic is being covered by another doctor for a while. With the help of a few nurses." He imparted that information as he reached for the handle of the bedroom door.

"What? How? Why?" Maddie knew she was babbling, but she didn't have a clue what he was saying.

He opened the door and turned, his expression dark, his eyes turbulent. "It was done on my orders, my arrangement."

"You can't just take over my clinic, Hudson. Or my life for that matter," she snapped at him, furious.

"Somebody needs to and I just did, Sunshine. And that's just the beginning. Meet me downstairs." He turned and left, pulling the bedroom door closed behind him.

Maddie was fuming as she entered the bathroom, tempted to chase Sam's ass down and tell him off. But she needed to prepare herself. He had her so angry right now that she wouldn't be at all effective at shooting him down in her current mood.

Who the hell was running her clinic? Were they taking good care of the people there? Dammit!

She stripped out of her scrubs and underwear, folding them together in a bundle to take with her when she left, which she planned to do immediately after she dealt with Sam Hudson.

It took her a moment to figure out how to use the fancy shower he had, one that had several showerheads that pulsated hot water over every muscle in her body, a decadent pleasure that made her bite back a moan as she washed her hair and scrubbed her body. Not at all surprised that he had female shower gel and shampoo in his shower, Maddie tried not to think about the gazillion women who had probably done more than just showered with Sam in this room, in this enclosure. Turning the shower off, she reached for a fluffy towel, patting her body dry and applying some lotion from the array of feminine toiletries lining the cupboards.

Clothing was piled on every surface, women's clothing. And every item still had the tags on them. Come to think of it, everything she had opened was brand new, including the shampoo and conditioner she'd used. Checking the size on a pair of jeans, she noticed that they were her size, as were all the clothes, every item a petite length. Even the new undergarments were her size—except none of the stuff was exactly her style. The underwear was decadent, wisps of silk and lace. The jeans were hip huggers, slimmer cut than she usually wore, cupping her curves and ass tightly when she slipped them on. Ignoring the image in the glass mirrors, she pulled a shirt over her head. It was a tee, but it was short and fit snugly over her breasts.

Oh, to hell with it. I'm changing at the clinic anyway.

She tamed her wild hair with a never-used hairbrush that she had to pull from the package.

No hair clips.

Scrounging through all the new lotions, gels, hairspray, and other assorted items, she found absolutely nothing to secure her riot of curls. With all of the attention Sam had paid to detail, Maddie knew it was intentional. He had never liked her hair pulled back.

Opening one of the medicine cabinets, she smiled evilly, yanking out a package of condoms.

Extra-Large.

Maddie would like to think that Sam having these was a case of wishful thinking, but she knew it wasn't. She'd felt that erection against her enough times to know he was built big.

Pulling one from the wrapping, she ripped off the top ring and trashed the rest of it in the garbage.

Perfect.

The band was stretchy enough to hold back her mass of curls in a ponytail at her neck.

Now all she needed was coffee and she'd feel human again. Grabbing her shoes from the side of the bed, she trotted down the stairs, having no idea where the kitchen was located. When she got to the bottom of the steps, she looked around, admiring the high cathedral ceiling and the light décor; the color scheme seemed to make everything seem lighter, more airy and cheerful.

She already knew Sam's home was massive, big enough to host a wedding and reception. Looking to the left, she saw a huge living room. On the right, she saw a massive entryway. Deducing that the kitchen was more likely to be to the right, Maddie wandered in that direction, eager to find a coffee maker. She needed her caffeine fix, and she needed it bad. Her headache had dulled to a slight annoyance, but her addiction to caffeine wasn't helping. Ignoring several smaller hallways, she followed what looked like a major corridor that might lead to the kitchen.

Yes! Finally!

There was a large arched doorway that led to a kitchen any professional chef would probably envy. And there, in front of the stove, stood Sam, his curls just starting to form as his hair dried, dressed in a snug pair of designer jeans and a polo shirt.

She watched as he filled two plates skillfully, like he actually cooked all the time. Her eyes darted nervously to her handbag that was sitting on the counter, and the paperwork she had carelessly stuffed inside the side pocket now resting underneath it.

She sidled up to the counter, sliding the paperwork from underneath her purse, folding it, and cramming it into the center part of the bag, closing the zipper tightly.

"I already saw them. The papers dropped out of your bag as I was bringing you into the house last night. I found them on the floor this morning." His voice was low, menacing.

"You read them?" Folding her arms in front of her, she scowled at him, resting one hip against the counter beside him.

"Not intentionally. But I opened them to see what they were. I thought they were papers that I'd dropped myself." He put the two plates on the kitchen table and pulled out one of the chairs. "You're not doing it, Maddie. Not now. Not ever," he told her adamantly. "Now eat." He sat a large mug of coffee beside her plate, the smell making her salivate.

"Actually, I'm not doing it. I can't afford it and it isn't fair to bring a child into the world just because I selfishly want one. I work horrible hours and it wouldn't be a good thing for a baby. I can adopt in the future. It was just a thought." She was thirty-four years old, would turn thirty-five this year. Artificial insemination had just been something she wanted to consider. She'd probably never marry, but she wanted a child so badly. She had actually hoped for more than one when she was younger.

She headed for the table, intent on grabbing the coffee. Before she had even taken a step, Sam snagged her arm, bringing her back against the counter, her ass pressed up against the unyielding wood as Sam slapped a muscular arm on each side of her, trapping her with his body. "Just tell me why? Why would you want to do that? Why aren't you married? Why don't you already have kids the normal way?" he growled, his intense eyes flashing as he looked down at her face, the muscles in his jaw clenched tightly.

She met his gaze with a fiery one of her own, her anger flaring as she retorted, "Because then I'd have to have sex and I don't like it."

"You don't like sex? Not with any of your partners?" he asked, his voice confused.

"Partner. As in one boyfriend. Tried it, didn't like it, didn't do it again. Lance said I wasn't a sexual woman and I probably have to agree with him. I had to have a few drinks just to let him do it."

"And you believed him? He told you the problem was yours, and you bought that, Maddie? It's crap. You're the sexiest woman I've ever known," he said in a husky voice. "And I know for a fact that you'd like sex. You just haven't had it with the right guy."

"Doesn't matter. No desire to try it again, which is why I was looking at artificial insemination," she answered, squirming to get away from him.

"If there's any inseminating to be done, I'm doing it. And it won't be done in a sterile environment with a Petri dish. All you need is a man who wants to please you to the point of insanity. And that would be me," he rasped, his mouth swooping down to capture hers.

Maddie pushed against his chest, frantic to get away, her heart skittering the moment his mouth captured hers. *Oh, God.* Yeah, Sam could set her on fire like no other man could with just his kiss, but the sexual act was a whole different thing. Her hands clenched his shoulders as he plundered, his tongue sweeping into her mouth with his bold kisses that always made her weak, unable to resist. She surrendered, pushing her tongue against his as he thrust into her mouth, over and over. Her pussy flooded as she moaned against his

lips, her entire being consumed by Sam as he claimed her mouth
with a dominance that took her breath away.

His endless kisses continued, one leading into the next, every
embrace more sensual. His big hands moved under her short t-shirt,
gliding along the skin of her back, her abdomen, and finally cupping
her breasts through her flimsy bra, drawing his thumbs over her
sensitive nipples, stroking over them roughly in slow, torturous
circles. Angling Maddie farther back, Sam's nimble fingers unclipped
the front-fastening bra, his rough fingers cupping her bare breasts,
worshipping them with his hands.

Yes. Yes. Yes.

Pulling his lips from hers, his breath coming in harsh pants, he
grunted, "Wrap your legs around my waist, Maddie."

So far gone, so wanting, she didn't think about giving him her
weight, she just did as she was told, wrapping her arms his neck and
locking her legs around his hips, grinding into his massive, hard cock
with abandon, moaning softly as she felt the friction against her clit.

Sam moved, stopping at the island breakfast bar and laying her
back on the cool tile. Her back supported, he swooped down and
feasted on her bare breasts, moving her t-shirt up and out of his
way. He cupped and tasted, bit gently and laved, until Maddie was
moaning his name. "Sam. Oh, my God, Sam."

Her head moved side to side, frustration building. *More.* She
needed more. Undulating her hips to get friction to her saturated
pussy, she ground against his rigid member, burning for release.

"You're fucking beautiful, Maddie. So aroused for me." His hand
slid to the button of her jeans, flipping it open, and lowering the
zipper. He leaned up slightly and she almost sobbed with disappointment as his mouth left her breasts. Until his hand slid between their
bodies and into her panties, his fingers boldly invading her drenched
folds to find her clit.

"Sam, I can't take it. I can't." Her head thrashed, back arching
as he circled the bundle of nerves, ramping up her desire until she
wanted to curse at him to make her come.

"You're so fucking wet. Take what you need," he told her harshly.

"I need you," she panted, suddenly realizing that she wanted that massive cock buried inside her, claiming her.

His fingers mastered her pussy, stroking over her bud with just enough pressure to drive her insane. "Climax, Maddie. I want to watch you come."

As though she were obeying his orders, she exploded as he increased the pressure of his fingers on her clit, making her shatter with a tortured moan.

Sam inserted one finger in her channel while he continued stroking her clit. "Fuck. I love feeling you come. I wish you were coming around my cock right now."

As her channel clenched around his finger, Maddie wished she was too. Her whole body trembled as she panted for breath, her heartbeat thundering in her ears.

Sam pulled his hand from her panties and jerked her against his chest. Her legs still clamped around his waist, she rested her head on his shoulder, wondering what in the hell had just happened. Sure, she had brought herself to climax before, but never like that. "Oh God, what have I done?" she whispered softly to herself, feeling a sense of impending doom, knowing her life would never be the same again.

Chapter 4

Obviously, Sam heard her hushed question. He pulled back, scowling at her. "You got off. Hard. So don't tell me you don't like sex, Maddie. You like it with me. Only with me." She pulled back and watched as he licked her cream from his fingers, his eyes closing, his face showing a look of complete ecstasy. "Fuck. I'll never be able to forget your smell, your incredible taste. I should have made you come with my mouth." He spoke between licks, the sight erotic as hell. "Now I want to taste you. All of you." Opening his eyes, he speared her with a look so hot that she creamed all over again, her panties saturated.

Squirming, she dropped her legs from his waist and pushed on his chest. Grabbing her ass, he gently lowered her to the floor, letting her slide down his aroused body slowly. Embarrassed, she quickly turned her back to him and fastened her bra and jeans, knowing she really needed to change her panties. "I'll be back," she mumbled, mortified and not sure what else to say.

"Hey." Sam caught her arm, bringing her around to face him. "You're blushing. You're not embarrassed, are you?"

She nodded.

"Why? Don't be. That was the most erotic thing I've ever seen," he told her, his hands stroking her bare arms up and down.

"I—I—don't do those sort of things. I don't react that way." Oh, shit. She was stammering. "We hate each other."

Grabbing her upper arms, he shook her lightly. "You may hate me, but I've never hated you, Maddie. Not ever." Leading her to a chair, he waved at the seat. "Sit. I'll nuke our food."

After retrieving some ibuprofen from her purse, she sat, her mind and body still stunned. Grabbing her coffee, she popped the pills for her headache and slugged down half of the lukewarm liquid before taking a break.

Moments later, Sam set the heated plates in front of them. "Eat something, Maddie. Do you want more coffee?"

She shook her head. "Maybe in a while."

He stood looking down at her for a moment before he started to finger her hair. He tugged at the elastic from his condom, a loud, masculine laugh escaping his mouth before he commented, "Very creative, Sunshine."

She looked up at him smugly. "I thought so. Glad you were an extra-large or it might not have been big enough to hold all my hair back."

"There are other advantages to that," he answered lightly as he seated himself.

She wasn't touching that comment. Watching him as he shoveled in his eggs, bacon, and potatoes ravenously, while still looking immaculate, Maddie never would have known that he had just given her the most incredible orgasm of her life with nothing more than his talented fingers and mouth.

She shuddered, picking up her fork with fingers that were slightly shaky. Starting slowly due to her lack of interest in food at the moment, she picked up speed, cleaning her plate quickly. "God, that was delicious. I didn't know you could cook."

He shot her a wicked grin. "You never asked. And I didn't have much to work with when we were together. Mom tried to teach both

Simon and me to cook. My lessons stuck and I learned to enjoy it. Simon's never did."

He'd really only had a hot plate because his stove didn't work in his small apartment back then. Still, he was pretty talented. It was the best breakfast she'd had in a while, even reheated. "Kara's terrified to let Simon into the kitchen." Maddie smiled, remembering two episodes where Simon had tried to cook. Both had been a nightmare, one episode triggering the fire alarms because of the smoke.

Sam dropped his fork and napkin onto the empty plate and picked up his coffee. "It's strange, because Simon's always been the creative one."

Maddie gaped at him as she picked up her mug. "That's not true. You're brilliant." Yeah, Sam might be a dog with women, but he was an incredible businessman. She'd followed the growth of his company, although she would never admit it. Sam had taken the business of developing Simon's computer games to a whole new level, and then proceeded to expand Hudson into commercial real estate and other ventures, making it one of the most diversified and powerful corporations in the world. Simon still headed the computer game development portion, but Sam was responsible for much of their billionaire status with the other ventures.

Sam shrugged. "I was just the go-to guy. Simon was the brains behind the company."

"You really think that? I know he did the initial designs, but who sold them, marketed them, who invested and started the other ventures? He may be the brilliant game developer, but you're the genius in business. It took both to make the company."

Sam took a slug of his coffee and lowered the mug to the table, shooting her an amused glance. "Madeline, if I didn't know better, I'd think you were throwing me a compliment."

Rolling her eyes, she got up and picked up the plates, rinsing them before putting them into the dishwasher. "I tell the truth as I see it. I may not like you for the most part, but I can't deny that you're successful." *Ridiculously so!*

Sam helped her load the remaining dishes. He refilled their coffee and set the mugs on the table. "We need to talk, Maddie."

"Actually, I need to get home. I need to get dressed and be back for the rehearsal," she told him lightly, not wanting to hear whatever he had to say. His tone was too serious, too much like the Sam she used to know, and it made her weak with longing, yearning for something that could never happen again.

"You have clothes here. Sit," he grumbled, his expression implacable.

Instead of sitting, she grabbed the coffee mug and took a sip, eyeing him cautiously. "Just tell me whatever you have to tell me. You have no say in my life and what I do, but I'll listen. Then I need to go." It seemed like the fastest way to get away from him. And she needed to remove herself from the presence of the hottest man she had ever known. Immediately.

"You aren't going anywhere today. Or tomorrow. Or the day after that," he growled, taking her coffee mug from her hand and sitting it back on the table. "You're taking some time off while you consider my proposition."

Crossing her arms in front of her, she mumbled, "And what is that?"

"I want you to leave your job at the hospital and work full-time at the clinic. As a paid physician. I'll start your salary at a half million a year and you can do all of your work in the daytime there. I want you out of there before dark and you can't work more than five days a week. It will give you more time there without the stress of having to juggle two jobs." He shot her an irritable look.

"It's a free clinic. I can't take a salary," she answered, perplexed.

"It's run on donations. I can up my donations and pay your salary myself. I have a lot of contacts who would be more than willing to help you back the clinic. All I have to do is call them." He raised an eyebrow, as though daring her to tell him differently.

Obviously, he did have contacts, other rich businessmen who could help fully fund her clinic. *Oh, God.* What would it be like to be able to be at the clinic every day, a place where she could really make a difference in people's lives? She liked her job at the hospital and it was fulfilling to take care of patients there, but it wasn't the same as helping people who couldn't afford healthcare. And there were plenty of other doctors who would take her job at the hospital. The clinic…umm…not so much.

"I'm not worth that much money. I'm just a family practice doctor. I don't earn that kind of salary." Seriously, was she really considering his offer? Shit! He was dangling a carrot that she almost couldn't refuse to take.

It's Sam Hudson, Maddie. Be careful.

Thing was, she didn't really *want* to be careful. She wanted to grab this opportunity. "What's the catch?" she asked cautiously. "There's nothing in it for you except a bigger tax deduction if you take it on as a charitable organization. Why put yourself to this much trouble for my clinic?"

"I get to know you're safe every day and out of the clinic before dark. I'll know you're sleeping, eating." He shrugged. "The conditions are firm. No working after dark and no more than five days a week."

He was manipulating her, and she didn't like it. However, it was hard not to accept when it was something she had always wanted. "Lower my salary. I'd rather use it to pay some full-time staff. I just need enough to pay my student loans and mortgage plus some other minor expenses."

"No. The salary gets paid and I'll pay your student loans off. I'll make sure your donations are enough to pay staff and buy state-of-the-art equipment." He crossed his arms in front of him, his face like granite.

They were negotiating, but Maddie felt like every time she opened her mouth he wanted to *do more.* "Why are you doing this? Really?"

"I'm doing it for you," he replied, his eyes boring into her. "And partly for myself," he admitted reluctantly.

"Are we signing contracts?" she asked, wanting to know she'd be legally protected. She wanted to believe that Sam was sincere, but she'd never be taken in by him again. One massive heartache was more than enough. He'd taken her trust once and smashed it to bits, making her suspicious of anything he offered.

"No. Not if you accept my entire offer," he rumbled, his voice husky.

"What else is there?" What more could he possibly offer?

"I want to get you pregnant," he said harshly. "You'll be in a position to have a baby and I want to be the one to do it. I don't want another man's seed inside your body."

Maddie gasped, her heart racing. Was the guy crazy? "You want to be my sperm donor?"

"Hell, no. Or yes…I do…but we do it the old-fashioned way. I'm willing to try for as long as it takes. Every day. Five times a day. Or until you beg for mercy, and even then I'm still not sure I'll stop." He pulled her into his body and unbound her hair, spearing his hands into the mass of curls possessively.

Maddie's mind whirled in confusion, her heart thudding against the wall of her chest so hard she swore it was going to burst through her sternum. "That takes having sex. A lot of sex. Unprotected sex." Oh, hell no. "I don't like sex and you're a man-whore, Sam. You couldn't go a week without another woman. I won't be enough for you. And I definitely don't want to share diseases with your lady friends."

Not happening. Having Sam Hudson as a father for the child I want so desperately has "complicated" written all over it.

"I'm clean. I'll give you my health records." Pulling back, he drilled her with those emerald eyes. They were tumultuous and stormy, as though he were holding himself in check.

"I can't. I trusted you once. I can't do it again. Especially not with a possible child involved," she answered sadly, her eyes starting to fill with tears. Incredibly, she almost wanted to agree. What would it be like to hold Sam's baby, *their baby*, in her arms? Need slammed into her so hard that she swayed. Not only did she want a baby, but she wanted Sam. Her problems with sex had nothing to do with her physiology. It all boiled down to him, to Sam. No other man had been Sam, so she hadn't wanted anyone else. When it came to sharing something that intimate, it only felt right with one person, a man who had broken her heart so many years ago.

I must be crazy, a freaking masochist, to feel this way.

"I haven't been with a woman in months. I fucking couldn't. Before that, I only slept with women who had red hair, curvy bodies and who didn't mind that I called out your name when I came," he snarled. "Women who only wanted money or material things, because I had nothing else to give them."

"Sam, you're with a different woman every week—"

"Friends who go with me to various functions. I don't sleep with them. I have no desire to sleep with a tall, skinny blonde. I'm too fucking obsessed with a petite redhead who hates me." He laughed, a humorless, self-deprecating laugh.

Oh Lord, was it really true? Still, he had cheated on her when they were dating. Like the proverbial leopard that couldn't change its spots, Sam couldn't have changed that much, could he? "I can't. It will never work. I can't sleep with you, get pregnant and walk away." *It would kill me!*

"If you fucking walked away, I'd come after you." His nostrils flared as he looked down at her with so much intensity that she could hardly hold his gaze.

"Then why did you even suggest it?" she asked curiously.

"I don't think you understand, Madeline. I'm not asking to just knock you up or fuck you, although God knows I want that too."

"What do you want?"

He took a deep breath, letting it out slowly, his whole body tense. "I want you to fucking marry me. I'm not asking for a few months of wild sex. I'm asking for forever. You, me, a family. Everything. Everything we should have had but didn't. I don't deserve you, but I fucking want you. So much it's killing me."

Sam took another deep breath…and waited.

Chapter 5

S am held his breath, watching Maddie's expression change to one of incredibility, as her mind tried to absorb what he'd just said. Shock. Disbelief. Horror. All of those emotions reflected back at him from her hazel eyes. Christ! He hadn't meant to say that. He hadn't meant to say *any* of it, except for the proposition to help her make her clinic a full-time paid venture to make her life easier. But then he'd seen those damn papers, and he'd completely lost it.

No man is planting his seed inside my woman, artificially done or not. If she wants a baby, I'll give her one or happily die trying.

Rampant, possessive emotions rose inside him until his vision blurred, his fists clenched with need to own the woman in front of him, a woman he'd wanted for what seemed like forever. The last time he had walked away from her, he had done it because he *thought* she'd be better off without him. *Fuck it.* He wasn't doing that again. She obviously wasn't happy, some guy had treated her like shit, and she didn't have the family she had always wanted. She was alone. Or, she *had* been alone. Now, Sam was determined that she would have *him*. Forever. Even if she hated him, he would treat her better than another man could, take better care of her, meet *all* of her needs until she begged for mercy.

Bullshit…she doesn't like sex! She had just never had a man who wanted to please her. Maddie was a firecracker that he wanted to set off. Hell…he wanted to do an entire fireworks display with her, one orgasm after another, until she begged him to stop, her body limp and sated.

Sam never saw the palm coming toward his face, his fantasies and desires so potent that he was lost in them. The *smack* landed hard enough to jerk his head to the right, and it was loud enough to be heard echoing through the kitchen.

"How could you? How could you play with me like this? You bastard, what did I ever do to you to deserve this?" Maddie hissed, her eyes furious and filled with tears. "I don't want to play your stupid games, Hudson."

Sam caught her wrist just as she was about to let her hand fly a second time. "No." He held her wrist tightly enough to immobilize it, but not enough to hurt. "I probably deserved what I just got for hurting you in the past. But I'm not taking another bitch-slap for offering to marry you and give you everything you want."

"You're a damn liar. You don't want to marry me or even fund my clinic. This is some kind of sick, twisted joke. And I don't understand why." Tears spilled from her eyes, eyes that were full of hurt and confusion.

"Goddamn it, Maddie." He swung her up into his arms. She kicked and twisted until he wrapped his arms around her, holding her immobile. "It's not a fucking joke. I'm not twisted. Much." Okay… maybe he was a little, but not about this, not about her.

Angry, he carried her to the living room, fuming. Dumping her on a roomy leather couch, he came down on top of her, restraining her flailing hands by holding her wrists above her head.

His chest heaving, Sam looked at her face, keeping most of his weight from her smaller frame with his legs. Tears were streaming from her eyes, an endless river that didn't seem to be stopping. *Fuck!* "Please don't cry, Maddie." *I can't handle it when she cries. She's had too much disappointment and pain in her life already.* Knowing he was the source of her tears, no matter how unintentional, nearly killed him.

She turned her face away from him. "Let go. I want to leave."

"The offer was sincere, Maddie. I'm not sure why you think I'd play that kind of game with you, but I have no reason to do that. Think about it. It makes no sense." He sighed, frustrated.

She turned her head and nailed him with a searching look. "About as much sense as you asking me to marry you. We hate each other—"

"You hate me. I don't hate you. I never have," he rasped, trying to squelch the barrage of emotions pounding at him.

"You didn't want to fuck me, either. And you didn't even respect me enough to break up with *me* before you fucked *her*. I cared about you, Sam. And seeing you with that woman made a mockery of everything we ever shared. Our friendship. Our relationship. Everything was just one big joke on me." She yanked at her hands, and Sam released her, sitting up to give her space since she appeared calmer.

"Maddie, I—"

"So excuse me if I think this is just another twisted lie, but I don't trust you. With good reason," she finished, running a shaky hand through her hair to thrust back her wayward curls from her face, her face still damp from spent tears. "I need to leave. Can you take me to the clinic to pick up my car?"

"No. You're staying. The rehearsal is starting in a few hours," he insisted, his jaw clenched. "You didn't give me an answer on my proposal."

"Because I don't think it's really necessary, but if you want one… then the answer is no. Hell no. Absolutely not," she gasped. "You broke my heart once. How stupid do you think I am? Unless you can give me a damn good reason why you were sucking tongue with that tall, skinny, beautiful woman all those years ago—"

"Because I didn't have a goddamn choice," he shouted hoarsely, the explosion coming from deep inside his body. "I had to get you away from me so you didn't get hurt. That woman, who was at least fifteen years older than me, was a fucking FBI agent. Did you even look at her?" He shuddered, his emotions close to the surface, unable to remember that nightmare day without nearly flying into a frustrated rage.

"All I remember is that she was pretty and she had her tongue down your throat. And your hands were all over her," Maddie answered, her voice uncertain, sad with remembered pain.

"She was good at her job. We were meeting to try to find a way to protect you. That's why I asked you to come and meet me for coffee. Kate said the best way to protect you was to alienate you, but I couldn't do it. I cared too damn much. She told me if I really cared about you, I'd worry about your safety first. She was right, but I didn't know how to walk away from you, even though I knew somehow I had to so I would know you were safe. So when she saw you coming, she did it herself by shoving her tongue down my throat. She convinced me that making you hate me was the way to save you, so yeah, I played into it. I didn't know whether to thank her or hate her fucking guts afterward. I hated having my hands on a woman who wasn't you, Maddie. I hated it while it was happening, knowing you were watching and feeling betrayed. And if you think I haven't lived with the regret of having to do that every fucking day since it happened...you'd be wrong."

Sam sat next to Maddie and buried his face in his hands, still hating himself for what had happened, but knowing that it *had* been the only way. Back then, he had been young and selfish, unable to push Maddie away because he wanted her too badly, needed her too much. And she was so loyal that she never would have left him unless she thought herself betrayed. "I didn't want to hurt you, but the thought of something happening to you made me so crazy that I did what I had to do."

"Why the FBI? Were you in some kind of trouble?" Maddie questioned, her voice still full of doubt and confusion.

He sat back on the couch, resting his head against the leather. "Not me. Not really. You know my history, Maddie. You know my father died of an overdose and that he had connections to organized crime."

"Yes," she nodded. "You told me. He died soon after we met."

"I knew things. Things that could help take the whole organization down. My father was not a nice man. I ran interference between the old man and Simon, doing whatever I had to do to keep the old bastard from hurting my little brother. I was underage when I ran errands and did other things under duress, so I wasn't really in trouble. But I also knew enough to help take down a worldwide organization that was pure evil."

He took a deep breath and blew it out before he continued. "I came here to Tampa just hoping to get my family away, to start a new life and just leave that life behind. But once I met you, I knew I couldn't bury all of my past and just run, pretend I didn't know things. I wanted to be a good man, and a decent person wouldn't be selfish enough not to try to prevent the pain and death caused by this organization. I had to do what I could to take the bastards down. I went to the Feds around December and fed them information, worked with them to help the investigation. It took months, but they finally got agents on the inside and enough information to bring the whole thing tumbling down. Unfortunately, information got leaked that I was a snitch, and that made me and anyone I cared about a target. Kate helped me realize I couldn't afford to be close to anyone. I was a dangerous person to know."

"I would have stayed with you, done whatever—"

"And you could have wound up dead. I couldn't take that chance." He sat up, grasping Maddie by the shoulders, shaking her lightly. "I didn't even get my mother and Simon out in time. Simon was stabbed by someone in the organization, a payback for my father being disloyal. Those were people who killed without a thought. They didn't give a shit about any human life. Do you understand?" he growled, his emotions ready to explode from his body. Perspiration poured down his face, a reaction he had every time he thought about what had happened to Simon and what could have happened to Maddie.

"What happened to Simon wasn't your fault, Sam," Maddie answered quietly, her voice soothing.

"Bullshit! I was his big brother. I should have gotten him out sooner. I should have known they'd take revenge on whoever was available." Releasing Maddie, he slumped back on the couch.

"You were barely an adult yourself. How could you have known?"

"I should have known. I'd seen these people in action since I could walk," he answered softly, dangerously.

"Why didn't you find me later? After the whole thing ended?" Maddie queried, her voice tremulous.

"It took over a year until every branch of the organization was closed down. My mother, Simon, and I were under FBI protection here in Tampa until every boss was behind bars or dead," he answered, his voice low and thoughtful.

"But after that, why didn't you find me?"

"I did." Sam clenched his fists, hating to think about the day he had gone to find her. He'd already known he had lost her, but that particular day was the time that it really sunk in, that he had to admit to himself that *his* Maddie was gone forever.

"I never saw you again," she answered, confused.

"I saw you. This time it was me who had to see you with another man with his tongue down your throat." He frowned, his face fierce. "I tracked you down on campus, but some dark-haired guy who looked like a jock was all over you. I thought you looked happy. He looked like he came from money and could make you happy. You'd moved on with your life and I couldn't blame you for finding someone better." *Fuck. That hurt.*

"Lance," she whispered. "We started dating a little over a year after what happened. You should have talked to me."

"Why? All it would have done is screwed up your life. I didn't have a fucking thing to offer, Maddie. I was barely out of danger from a lengthy FBI involvement. Broker than shit from trying to support my family. Simon was going to school. I stopped so he could study. Once he was old enough to work part-time, I went back to finish my own degree. You had a guy who looked like a much better option than me back then." Maddie would never know how hard it had been to walk away, to leave her in the arms of another man. But Kate had been right when she said if you really care about someone you do what's best for them. "Had I known that he was a bastard who wasn't going to marry you and who treated you poorly, I would have taken you away from him in a fucking heartbeat. I assume that he was the one sexual relationship you mentioned? That guy was the son of a bitch who told you that you weren't sexy?" God, what he wouldn't do to have his hands around the asshole's neck right now. He hated himself for leaving his precious Maddie in the care of someone who didn't deserve her.

"Yeah. We didn't really date that long. Six months." She shuddered as she looked up at Sam, the pain in her eyes almost tangible. "I was so lonely and I wanted to forget you."

"And you haven't tried again since then?" he asked, his voice gentler, curious.

Maddie shook her head. "No. I've dated casually, but there was... nothing."

Sam reached out his hand and captured one of the tears on her cheek with his finger and brought it to his lips. "Jesus, Maddie. I can't imagine any man letting you get away."

"Except you." She smiled sadly.

"You haven't gotten away from me yet, and this time you won't," he answered harshly. "I want you to marry me."

Sam looked at the agonized expression on her face and it nearly brought him to his knees. He needed her to say yes. Desperately. His sanity was beginning to depend on it.

"We don't even know each other anymore. I don't know what to say right now," she told him honestly.

"Say yes."

Oh, fuck yeah. Saying no was *not* an option. Sam moved her onto his lap. He needed to hold her right now, had to have her softness in his arms.

She squealed and tried to squirm away, but he didn't let her. "Either sit quietly or I'll have you on your back and moaning within a few seconds," he warned her ominously. "I can't handle much of that delicious ass squirming on my cock before I tear those sexy clothes from your body and taste every inch of you."

She stilled immediately and wrapped her arms around his neck. "What happened to Kate?" she asked curiously, resting her head on his shoulder.

Sam shrugged. "I don't know. I never saw her again after the investigation. She was married. Happily married with two kids. She had no desire to mess with me. I was a dumb kid to her. It was all a ruse that she executed to force me to cut things off with you." He thrust a hand into her hair, massaging her scalp. "So, what's your answer, Maddie?"

"Sam, I haven't even digested the information you just told me. You can't expect me to agree to marry you." She pulled back and shot him a disgruntled look.

"If you don't believe me, you can ask Simon. He doesn't know about us, but he can verify everything else," he told her, disappointed that she might not believe him after he had bared his soul to her.

"It isn't that. I just need time." She sighed. "It's been years, Sam. We've changed. We don't know each other now."

"We've always known each other, Sunshine. My soul recognized yours the moment I saw you." And it was the truth. It hadn't taken him more than a moment to see her value, to know that she was special. "Fine, tell me yes tomorrow then." He was feeling magnanimous now that he had her exactly where he wanted her.

Maddie snorted. "That's very kind of you, but I think I may need a little longer than that."

Tilting her face, he speared her with a possessive glance. "How much longer?"

"I don't know," she whispered, her eyes sad.

Dammit! He didn't want her dejected. He wanted her to want him. No…he needed her to want him. "I'll seduce you. Then I'll fuck you until you don't have the strength to say anything except yes. No one is planting their seed inside you except me."

Maddie rolled her eyes. "Nobody has ever planted their seed inside me. Lance used a condom and I haven't had anything but my vibrator since."

Something raw and carnal nailed Sam in the gut, the thought of Maddie pleasuring herself making his already-rigid cock jump, feral instinct making him want to be the first to release himself into her womb. He had never had sex without a condom. In that way, Maddie would be his first, his only since he never planned to be with any other woman again. "And how's the vibrator?" he choked out, barely able to form the words.

She shrugged, giving him a sweet smile. "Batteries are probably dead. It's been a while."

Christ! She was fucking killing him. "You won't need it," he rasped, burying his face in the silken skin of her neck.

She tilted her head, giving him better access as she murmured, "Is it true that you didn't go to bed with all those women?"

"What I said is true. I know what the gossip columns say and what people think, but it's not true. The women people see me with are nothing more than friends or acquaintances, women who want to attend the parties. I won't claim to be a saint, Maddie. I've fucked. But none of them were you," he answered, his voice husky against her skin.

"I missed you. I missed you so much," she replied, her voice filled with pain and sadness.

Unable to stop himself, Sam slipped Maddie off his lap and under him, covering her petite body with his larger frame. She felt so sweet, so soft beneath him that he groaned as she opened her thighs to welcome him, and he felt like he was finally home, exactly where he was supposed to be. The feel of her body, her enticing fragrance surrounded him, sinking into his every pore. "I missed you, too, Sunshine. More than you can possibly imagine," he answered gruffly, lowering his body to hers while keeping most of his weight off her with his elbows, needing all of her softness. He buried his face in her silky curls, letting himself completely absorb her, breathing her in over and over again until every part of him was filled with her scent.

Mine. Need her. She'll never have another man as long as I'm breathing.

A low, incoherent sound left his throat, feral and unrestrained. "I'll never let you go. You can say yes today or tomorrow, but you'll always be mine."

He lowered his mouth to hers before she could reply, swallowing any protest she might have made. He didn't give a shit what words left her mouth; he was taking what should have been his years ago. Maybe he should have confessed everything the first time he had seen her again last year, but he hadn't gotten close to her, afraid that she had a man in her life, a man who was better for her than him. Now that he knew the truth, that she had never been cherished as she should have been, he wasn't letting her go.

She tasted of sweet coffee and raw temptation, and it nearly drove him mad. He covered her mouth over and over, trying to brand her as his, needing her to forget every man in the world except him. His cock pulsated and he thrust his pelvis into her core, groaning into her mouth as he was greeted with nothing but heat and the promise of ecstasy. He snaked his forearms under her back, trying to pull her closer, her breasts tighter against his chest. Fuck! He needed more. More of her, more of her heat. She moaned into his mouth as he plundered again, sweeping his tongue into the wet, warm cavity, greedy for her sweetness, wallowing in her essence.

Pulling his mouth from hers, he rasped, "Have to get closer. Naked. Now."

"Sam, someone is at the door. I heard the doorbell," Maddie panted softly.

Shit! Simon.

He looked at the clock and then back at Maddie, so damn tempted to ignore the penetrating ring of the doorbell again.

Maddie looked so warm, so soft, so ready to be fucked that he raked his hand through his hair in frustration. "Christ. It's Simon." He gave her a heated stare. "We finish this later."

Maddie sat up, pushing him off her gently. "Not happening. They're staying until Saturday, right?"

"Yeah. So?" Sam didn't care if they stayed, as long as he had Maddie with him.

"I'm not sleeping in your bedroom while they're here." Maddie scowled at him. "This is their wedding, Sam. I'm not doing anything that will cause talk. They deserve this time. And I know I need some time to think." She ran a hand through her hair, but it only made her curls wilder.

Sam's eyes raked over her disheveled appearance with male satisfaction. She looked like a woman who had just been ravished. "You don't need to think. You just need to say yes," he replied belligerently.

Maddie jumped up from the couch and gathered her hair in a ponytail. "I need my rubber."

Sam looked at her sardonically. "That just doesn't sound right coming out of a woman's mouth. In the kitchen. I'll get it."

"No. I'll get it. You get the door. Poor Simon and Kara are standing on the doorstep, probably wondering where you are."

"I was about to get luckier than I've ever been in my entire fucking life. Perfect timing, bro," Sam grumbled, heading for the door.

Maddie giggled, covering her mouth to stifle the sound. "I do need a few things from my house. And some fresh batteries," she told him as she sashayed across the room.

Sam groaned, watching her prance to the kitchen, that sweet ass wiggling enticingly as she went, in a pair of jeans he never should have asked David to buy. They were too provocative, cupped her ass too perfectly.

Batteries? Why did she need—?

Oh shit. How screwed could one man get? He smirked as he moved toward the front door. Point scored by Maddie. And he would give her this one. Because, in the end, he planned to win by a landslide.

He put his hand on the doorknob, trying to adjust his throbbing erection before he opened it, and attempting to banish visions of Maddie pleasuring herself with her vibrator.

"You'll pay for this one, Sunshine," he whispered to himself with a small smile as he pulled open the door.

Sam had waited forever for Maddie, but suddenly, he just couldn't wait any longer. He was being given a second chance, and this time he wasn't letting her go, because nobody else in the world needed her as much as he did. And nobody would treasure her as much as he would.

His resolve and his cock hard as steel, he smiled broadly as he greeted Simon and Kara.

Chapter 6

Maddie cried at the wedding. She couldn't help herself. It wasn't possible to watch Simon and Kara exchange vows without tears of joy cascading from her eyes, her happiness for her friend nearly painful. As the couple faced each other, Maddie watched Simon's face, Kara's back to her as she recited her vows to her almost-husband. Every emotion was raw and unguarded on Simon's face as he repeated his vows gruffly, but with tender emotion.

She and Sam were the only attendants, the small audience made up of friends and family. The weather had cooperated so everything had been set up outdoors, and the decorations were exquisite. Kara had opted for a small ceremony, although there was a lavish reception planned for after the wedding when hundreds of people would gather in Sam's elegant home to give their best wishes to the happy couple.

Kara looked like a princess in her ivory Victorian gown of silk and the finest lace. The style suited Kara, who was tall and svelte; the gown was fitted until it reached her hips and then flared in a bell to the floor.

Maddie adored her own emerald green, tea-length dress with its off-the-shoulder, short bell-sleeves and plunging neckline, a daring bodice that had made her shudder when she'd first seen it. But after she had tried it on, she'd fallen in love with the fitted waist and billowy skirt that hit her below the knee. The outfit was accented with a black silky tie belt that floated behind her in shimmering waves. The ensemble was finished with black, strappy heels, and Maddie knew she looked as good as she could manage when standing next to a tall and stunning woman like Kara.

Maddie looked across the happy couple at Sam, who was absolutely breathtaking. Simon was in an identical black tux, but Simon was wearing a bow tie. Sam was wearing a thin black tie with tiny stripes of emerald green that matched her dress...and his gorgeous eyes. Everything about him looked urbane and sophisticated, right down to his stance and expression, a man obviously completely comfortable in his surroundings and attire.

Forcing herself to tear her eyes away from Sam, Maddie returned her gaze to Simon, watching him pledge himself to Kara.

When the minister reached the part of the ceremony where he asked if anyone had any objections, Simon scowled.

Turning his head briefly toward the man of the cloth, Simon informed the minister irritably, "She's mine. Move on."

Maddie bit her lip to keep from giggling. Simon Hudson was far from subtle about his possessiveness of Kara. Her eyes met Sam's and her heart skittered. She could tell he was stifling a grin and his eyes were dancing with amusement. Their eyes locked and held, sharing a brief moment of silent communication, of shared mirth.

Finally, as she wrenched her gaze from Sam, she felt a cold shiver run down her spine, the sense of another set of eyes on her. She was at a wedding with at least fifty guests. People were watching. But she turned her head and her eyes clashed with a man in the first row, a dangerous-looking man in an expensive suit staring directly at her, his eyes never leaving her face. The man was handsome in a rugged, intense sort of way, with auburn hair and laser-sharp eyes, eyes that bored into her with a look of intense concentration. Unable to look away, compelled to keep her eyes on him, Maddie was startled when his lips suddenly broke into a grin and he winked, actually winked...

at her. Really, there was something so magnetic about him that she couldn't help smiling back.

Turning her attention back to Simon and Kara, she watched through eyes blurred with tears as the minister pronounced them man and wife. Simon kissed his bride…and kissed his bride again… and finally stopped when Sam slapped him on the back in congratulations, but Maddie knew it was really to keep Simon from devouring his new wife in front of the guests. Kara's eyes were sparkling with tears as she hugged Maddie and took back her bouquet. Sam offered his arm and Maddie clenched it, following the newly-married couple down the aisle.

"I saw Max fucking you with his eyes. Don't even think about it," Sam rumbled under his breath, smiling broadly for the crowd while he said it.

"Who's Max?" she asked, confused, as she took his escort behind Kara and Simon.

"Maxwell Hamilton. The bastard who was checking you out in the front row. He couldn't take his eyes off you. Not that I blame him. But he better stay the fuck away from you or I'll kill him," Sam growled as they reached the end of the aisle. He wrapped a possessive arm around her waist, pulling her into his body.

Maddie had never met him, but she'd heard of him. Max Hamilton was another man who showed up in the gossip pages far too often because of his wealth and power. "You're obviously friends. He's here."

"Yeah, he's a friend, but right now I don't like him. I don't like the way he was eyeing you," he answered briskly. "We do a lot of business deals together."

The wedding had broken up and people were making their way to the lovely tents that were set up at the waterfront with tables of food, a bar, and a monstrous cake. The sun was beginning to set and the reception area took on a fairytale appearance. Maddie took a deep breath of the salty, humid air, enjoying the mild evening. "Everything looks so beautiful," she sighed.

"Yeah. Everything. You look breathtaking, Maddie. Did I tell you that?" Sam's gaze was trained on *her*, his eyes moving over her, lingering at the plunging neckline of her dress.

"Once or twice," she answered, blushing as he continued to stare. Actually, he'd told her at least five times since she had come down the stairs to make her way to the area where the ceremony was being held, and her face had flushed every damn time. It wasn't the words that Sam said; it was the way he said them. He might as well have told her that he needed to fuck her or die, so needy was his tone, the timbre of his voice sending chills down her spine and moisture to her pussy.

"How do you wear a bra with this dress?" he asked, his voice husky and desperate as he fingered the delicate sleeve.

"I don't," she whispered back to him, giving him a look of feigned innocence. "It's not possible."

A deep, vibrating groan came from his throat, sending a thrill to her core. Only with Sam had she ever felt this kind of feminine power, and it was heady.

"Jesus, Maddie. I'm already tied in knots from the last few days. I don't know if I can take much more." His jaw was clenched tightly. "For God's sake, don't bend over. Every male at the reception will be salivating. Fuck! I need a drink."

He took her hand, his grasp completely encapsulating her smaller one, and twined his fingers through hers in a proprietary way that had her heart leaping with joy. Every one of the wedding preparations had gone incredibly smoothly, everything perfectly planned. All the wedding party had to do was enjoy the festivities. Watching Simon and Kara together for the last few days had been achingly poignant, but satisfying. Maddie had no doubt that her friend would be happy with Simon. The two of them were like two parts of a whole, so happy together that it was almost painful to watch. Kara had been through so much, suffered for so much of her life alone. Maddie was grateful that Kara finally had a man who would make her ecstatically happy. Her friend was pregnant, but not enough to be showing yet. Although Maddie hadn't thought it possible, it had made Simon even more protective and nurturing with Kara. They would both make good parents. Any child born to the two of them would be blessed.

Sam tugged her hand, leading her toward the luxurious silk tent closest to the water. "Sam, slow down. Heels," she reminded him as she yanked on his hand, pointing at her feet when he turned. They were walking across the lawn, and she wasn't used to stiletto heels. If he didn't slow it down, she was going to turn her damn ankle.

He looked at her remorsefully. "Sorry, Sunshine. I forgot how petite you are." He scooped her up in his arms and cradled her close to his chest. "Problem solved," he said, shooting her a wicked grin. "I like this better anyway."

"Put me down," she hissed, mortified. "Everyone is watching." Swatting Sam was completely useless. Her hand bounced off the powerful muscles of his arms like she was smacking at solid rock. It hurt her palm more than it bothered him.

He strode toward the tent, ignoring her. "Let them watch," he answered, unconcerned.

"Damn it, Sam. Are you trying to cop a feel?" she asked, her expression admonishing, but she could barely contain a smile. One muscular arm was under her knees, but it encircled her legs, his palm caressing her thigh under the flimsy skirt of her dress.

"Yep. I'm trying to get a look down that skimpy bodice, too. A guy takes what he can get when he's desperate." He shot her a cocky look and then returned to leering at her breasts in a proprietary way that had her whole body tingling.

Maddie sighed, inhaling deeply, letting his masculine scent drift over her senses. *God, he smells so good.* Closing her eyes for just a moment, she let the impact of Sam seep into her being, her arms closing around his shoulders and fingering his silky curls at the nape of his neck. Being close to him again, feeling his rock hard body against hers was completely decadent. Everything about Sam drew her to him, made her want to sink into him, be joined to him. It was a carnal feeling, and one that she never felt with any other man. As if Sam were emitting male pheromones, and she wasn't capable of ignoring the masculine, enticing beckoning of her senses.

"What are you thinking about?" he asked in a low, seductive voice.

Maddie opened her eyes and stared at him. "You," she answered honestly.

His eyes grew intense and his grip tightened around her body. "If you don't stop looking at me like that, I'm taking you into the house, stripping you naked and fucking you until you beg me to stop. And then I'll do it all over again," he warned hoarsely.

She let that masculine warning slide over her, loving his intensity. Right now, there was nothing she wanted more than to call him on his threat. But she knew he'd follow through. "Simon's wedding reception," she reminded him. "Put me down."

He lowered her to the ground, keeping her gown around her legs so she was decent. "I don't want to let go." He guided her feet to the floor, but kept his arms around her.

Maddie didn't need Sam to explain because she knew exactly how he felt. Being together again was almost like a dream that she didn't want to end. They had always fit together like two puzzle pieces that locked into place when they were together, so natural that it was almost frightening. "I think I need that drink you were talking about." She needed something, anything, to make herself loosen her hold on Sam.

"What do you want?" he questioned, releasing his hold on her with a pained expression.

You. Inside me. Now.

"I'm not familiar with drinks. You choose." She smoothed the wrinkles from her dress as she licked her dry lips.

He put a hand on the small of her back, leading her to an elegant vacant table. After seating her with manners that any mother would be proud of, she watched him walk toward the bar, so parched, her tongue was sticking to the roof of her mouth. Sam had always done that to her. One look, one touch, one kiss…and she was captivated.

"Hello," a low baritone said casually above her.

Craning her neck, she saw the same man who had winked at her earlier during the ceremony, a broad smile on his charming face. And he *was* a charmer. Maddie was certain of that. He looked like the type of guy who could get himself out of any sticky situation, even if caught red-handed. "Hi," she answered cautiously.

"Max Hamilton. I wanted to meet you." He held out a friendly hand.

Maddie clasped it. "Maddie Reynolds. Nice to meet you, Mr. Hamilton."

"Please, call me Max," he said suavely, pulling his hand from hers and seating himself across from her. "Dr. Reynolds? Kara and Simon speak highly of you."

"Call me Maddie." She searched his face, looking into his gold-green eyes, checking for any signs of malice. There were none. She wasn't sure why Sam had been so hostile about this man. He seemed pretty harmless and very friendly. There was something about his smile that she liked, something about *him* that she liked.

"Beautiful wedding," he commented casually, his lips curling up in a small grin.

"Beautiful couple," Maddie added, returning his smile.

"You and Kara both look lovely, Maddie."

She cocked her head and looked at him, wondering why a guy like him wasn't with a woman. He was ruggedly handsome and, she knew, loaded. "I take it you didn't bring a date. I didn't see you with anyone." During the ceremony, he had been sitting next to an older gentleman and a woman old enough to be his grandmother.

He shook his head slowly, his auburn hair bright in the candlelit room. "No. I was married. I lost her two years ago."

"I'm sorry." Maddie suddenly wished she hadn't asked. His face grew pensive and sad.

"What about you? No husband? No boyfriend? Are you and Sam an item? You looked pretty friendly a while ago," he observed, his voice amused.

"I don't know," she answered truthfully.

"Would you have dinner with me, Maddie?" he asked, his expression earnest.

There was something in his eyes, something in his voice that made her want to say yes. Maybe it was the emptiness she saw in his expression or a loneliness she sensed behind his rather mysterious exterior. "Yes. Of course, that would be lovely." It was only dinner, so she had no reason to refuse.

"Give me your number." He pulled out his cell.

She rattled it off, finishing just as Sam stepped back to the table with their drinks.

Max smiled, depositing his cell back into his pocket and standing. "Sam. How are you?"

Sam's face was like stone, his expression grim. "I was fine until you started hitting on my woman," he answered gruffly as he plopped the drinks on the table and faced Max.

"Jesus. Don't go caveman on me, Sam. I was just introducing myself." Max took a step, as though he were ready to face off with Sam.

"Did you give him your phone number?" Sam growled, shooting Maddie a disapproving look.

"Sit down, Sam. Max, it was nice meeting you." She smiled at Max and gave Sam a warning look.

"You too, Maddie." Max shook her hand again and leaned down beside her ear to ask in a low, concerned voice, "You okay? He looks pissed off."

She rolled her eyes. "He usually does. I'm fine."

"I'll talk to you later." Max walked away, Sam giving him a belligerent look that said he would be willing to go rounds with him as he left.

Sam's eyes bored into Max's back, his fists clenched. He sat and knocked back half of his drink before he spoke. "You are not going anywhere with him." His fingers clenched around the glass, his eyes furious.

Maddie glanced at him and took a sip of the creamy white drink he had brought for her. "Umm…that's good. What is it?"

"White Russian," he answered briskly. "Did you hear me, Madeline?"

"I'm ignoring you until you do something other than give me orders. I don't like it." She took a larger sip of her drink, enjoying the smooth taste on her tongue.

"Hamilton is no good for you, Maddie. He's never gotten over his late wife. He'd make you miserable," he growled, tossing back the rest of his drink.

"He looks so lonely," she answered sadly.

"He is and I'm sorry for his pain, but you aren't the answer," he said huskily. "You're already taken by a man who needs you desperately. You're mine, Sunshine. You always have been."

She looked into Sam's gorgeous eyes and fell into their depths, completely unable to deny that she belonged to him. His look was both forlorn and fierce, the two combining until she wanted to cling to him and try to make his pain go away. "You can't just give me orders and expect me to blindly obey, Sam. I make my own decisions. I always have. I'm not the naïve young woman you once knew." She sipped at her drink, watching him with total fascination.

She could see a fine mist of perspiration coating his face, his barely leashed emotions close to the surface. He stood and grasped her hand, pulling her to her feet.

"Let's go dance." It wasn't a request. It was a statement.

Maddie sat her nearly empty glass on the table and followed him.

Chapter 7

Dancing with Sam was like making love on a dance floor. He touched, he caressed, he seduced, he whispered naughty things in her ear until her body was on fire and her panties were completely drenched. By the time they left the dance floor after several songs, Maddie was practically panting.

Kara cut her beautiful cake, and tossed her bouquet, which seemed to fly straight to Maddie, although she wasn't even trying to catch it. Simon didn't even bother to toss Kara's garter; he took it off his new bride in private and stuffed it into Sam's pocket with an evil grin. Surprisingly, Sam accepted it with a broad smile and a clap on the back to his younger brother, leaving a perplexed look on Simon's face.

"Our duty is done. Let's take a walk," Sam said in a graveled voice as he stood next to her, both of them sipping another drink and watching people slowly leaving the reception.

Maddie didn't ask where they were going. She didn't care. Her hand slipped into his comfortably and she followed wherever he wanted to lead.

He walked slowly across the lawn, letting go of her hand and wrapping an arm around her waist as they started down a cobbled pathway, nodding to a Hudson security agent at the head of the path.

"Nobody else comes down here tonight," Sam instructed the agent in a low voice as he guided Maddie around the older man.

"Yes, Mr. Hudson. I'll make sure they don't," the guard answered.

It was dark, probably unlit to keep guests away from areas where Sam didn't want them. Maddie gasped in delight as they exited the path, the moonlight illuminating the private dock and the water from the bay, an amazing sight with its distant points of light and the beauty of the stars. "It's beautiful. Is this your dock?"

"Yes. It's mine and it's private," he answered ominously.

Maddie stepped onto the dock, careful that her heels didn't catch in the slats. "So this is where you propositioned Kara?" she asked, trying not to sound jealous because Sam had once hit on her friend.

"It wasn't Kara I wanted. I was drunk and probably envious of how happy Simon looked. I didn't know how serious he was about her and had I not been drinking it never would have happened," he answered, as he swung Maddie up in his arms. "Even if she had agreed, it still wouldn't have happened. I was much too drunk to perform that night and once I was sober, I wouldn't have wanted to be with her. She's not my type."

She wanted to object to Sam carrying her, taking her weight, but he didn't look in the least bit stressed, striding down the walkway to a structure farther down the wooden dock. She wrapped her arms around his neck and put her head on his shoulder, knowing she could get used to this so very easily. Sam was such a hot alpha male who called to everything feminine inside her that she just wanted to melt into him, let him protect her for a while. "What is your type?" she questioned curiously.

"A petite, beautiful redhead who likes to tease," he replied gruffly, reaching the structure and bolting up a set of stairs.

Maddie's mouth opened in shock as he reached the top, pushing open a screen door with his shoulder. The upper floor was screened to keep bugs away, and one entire wall was made of glass, providing an awesome view of the water. "This is incredible," she whispered as Sam lowered her feet to the ground.

Obviously, someone had been expecting him. The place was decorated in all-weather patio furniture, but there were candles lit on every table and a bottle of champagne sat on ice with two fluted glasses next to a huge, cushy double lounger.

"I spend a lot of time here. It's quiet and peaceful," Sam said casually, pulling his tuxedo jacket off and throwing it on a chair. "I like the water."

"But you don't have a boat?" Maddie asked him, noticing the absence of any vessel attached to the dock.

He shrugged as he flopped into the lounger. "Never needed one. I can be on the water right here." He opened his arms to her. "Come here. I want to discuss your little comment about batteries, and how that's affected me for the last few days."

Maddie bit her lip nervously. Really, what Sam meant was that he wanted revenge, a reciprocation that would probably involve breath-stealing kisses and erotic torture.

She shot a quick glance at the door.

"Don't even think about it. I can be up and catching you within seconds, especially in those shoes," he commented reasonably, but with an underlying dangerous tone. "Either come to me or I'll come get you."

She sighed, knowing she didn't really want to get away. Slipping her feet out of her shoes, she slid into the lounger and was immediately encircled by strong arms that held her tightly against an equally muscular chest. "You're so bossy," she told him in a disgruntled voice.

"I always have been. You're just noticing that now? Simon started accusing me of it from the time he could speak," he retorted with laughter in his voice.

Actually, Sam's take-charge manner was something that she had always admired about him, but now he took being authoritative to a whole new level. She supposed it had a lot to do with his success. "You're different now," she mused. He was cultivated and cultured, but she wasn't so sure he had changed all that much on the inside. He was still as rough around the edges emotionally as he was back then. He just had learned to cover it in a bland, smooth exterior.

"Is that good or bad?" he asked, his hand sliding up and down her bare arm, leaving goose bumps on her flesh.

"Neither," she answered, fairly certain that underneath the glitz and wealth, he was pretty much the same man. That fact was both terrifying and comforting.

"How have the new batteries been working out for you, Madeline?" he asked in a hoarse, low voice.

She snorted as she fingered his tie. "They were very…um…stimulating, thanks."

"I had to fight with myself every night not to pound down the door of the guest bedroom, strip you naked and fuck you until you screamed with pleasure. I stroked myself off every night thinking about you pleasuring yourself." His voice sounded desperate, and he pulled the tiny sleeve of her dress lower. "Then today, I had to try to hide my erection all afternoon and evening when I saw you in this *fuck-me* dress, especially once I knew your breasts were bare, just waiting to be touched by my fingers, my mouth." The bodice started to slip as he inched the dress down farther. His hand entered the bodice from the side, pushing his way between the material and her bare breast.

Maddie's core flooded with heat, her nipples already hard and sensitive from his erotic words. She gasped as he cupped her breast possessively, lightly pinching her nipple. "Sam," she murmured in a needy voice she barely recognized as her own.

He rolled her beneath him in a smooth maneuver that left her staring up at him longingly. Her breath hitched as she saw the hunger and need shining in those emerald eyes above her, a sight she had wanted to see for so very long from this one man, an erotic fantasy come true. "You're mine, Madeline. You always have been and always will be. You might make me lose my fucking mind, but at least I'll be happily insane."

Yes. Yes. Yes.

Her whole being craved Sam Hudson, and only him. His domination aroused her; his scent enveloped her in carnal desire. "Then take me, Sam." No more waiting, no more questioning; there was only this man for her. He had always been the only one.

"You're going to marry me, Maddie. Promise me you will," he demanded, his hands pulling the sleeves down her arms, lowering the top half of her dress until her breasts sprang free, leaving her arms trapped to her sides by the straps he had lowered.

"I'll think about it," she agreed, moaning as his mouth lowered to her breasts, his hands pushing them together so he could switch from one breast to the other easily. His mouth bit gently at one nipple, and then suckled it erotically before switching to the other. Back and forth, over and over, until Maddie was out of her mind from the pleasurable torment.

"Promise," he commanded, flicking her nipple with his tongue.

She undulated her hips, thrusting her core against his hard erection, needing friction, needing to be filled, needing all of him. "For God's sake, just fuck me. We can talk about everything else later," she told him vehemently as she yanked her arms outward, tearing the small sleeves without an ounce of regret, in order to free her hands to be able to touch him.

Her hands speared through his curls, holding his head against her breast, urging him to give her more. Moving her trembling fingers down his back, she wrapped her legs around his waist and ground her pelvis against his groin, desperate.

Lifting his head from her breast, Sam took her mouth, a dominant claiming that had her moaning against his thrusting tongue and grinding her saturated pussy harder against his cock. His embrace was wild and rampant: his hands holding the back of her head, his desperate fingers making the clips in her hair fly away, keeping her still for his possession. Their tongues tangled in a hungry duel, both wild and untamed.

With a tormented, masculine groan, Sam came to his knees. He ripped off his tie and vest, tearing the buttons off without even taking the time to unfasten them. His shirt followed in the same manner, all of the discarded items hitting the floor without a care. Maddie sat up from her reclining position and Sam immediately grasped the zipper on the back of the dress, lowered it and tugged the dress to her hips and then down her thighs as she lifted her ass for him to remove it.

"Christ, Maddie! You are the most beautiful sight I've ever seen. Nothing even comes close," he growled, standing to discard the rest of his clothing. His eyes never left her body as she reclined again. He stared blatantly as he removed his pants, socks, and boxers, his eyes emanating liquid desire.

She gaped as she saw his cock standing erect and enormous against his ripped abs, her empty pussy clenching with need. Sam had a body that probably haunted every woman's fantasies. Big, muscular, and perfect. For her, he was the whole package; he was *her* Sam all over, including the intent, erotic look that he was shooting her from those intense eyes.

Always body conscious, she should have been embarrassed, but she wasn't. Sam liked her curvy body and she was in excellent aerobic shape, working out several days a week. Seeing the look on his face, she didn't regret a single curve at the moment. He obviously appreciated her rounded hips and larger than average breasts. He made her feel like a sex goddess, a very unusual and erotic feeling for her.

"Come," she begged him, her arms reaching for him. She needed to feel his body against hers, filling her.

"No. You come first," he told her wickedly, intentionally misunderstanding her meaning. "I've been dying to taste you and I will."

Crawling up the lounger, he settled between her thighs, spreading her legs wide. She was wearing wispy green panties and a pair of nude thigh-high stockings with scalloped lace at the top.

Suddenly nervous, she stammered, "Sam, I-I've not...I don't...I—"

"You've never let a guy go down on you?" he grumbled, his fingers delicately stroking the strip of skin exposed at the top of her thigh.

"No one ever asked," she moaned, as his tongue replaced his fingers, laving the flesh at the top of her thigh in slow, sensual strokes.

"Good," he answered with male satisfaction. "And I'm not asking, Sunshine. I'm taking what's mine. What's always been mine."

She was rendered mute as he licked teasingly over the barely-there panties, stroking over her wet folds through the thin fabric. Trembling, she fisted her hands into his hair, not at all certain that she could take much more teasing. "Please, Sam. I need you."

"You have me, Maddie. You always have," he answered huskily against her mound.

Her panties broke away with a sharp tug and a tearing sound that made her feel only relief, one step closer to their joining. The first touch of his mouth was agony and ecstasy, the sensation unlike anything she had ever felt before. Suddenly, she was glad Sam was the first to do this, the act so intimate that it would have been a sacrilege with anyone else. But not with Sam, never with him. The only thing she felt with Sam was the need for more. She massaged his scalp with a needy moan as his tongue bathed her from bottom to top, hesitating around her clit, circling it until she wanted to scream.

"Please. Please." She begged as she panted, her back arching as his fingers joined his mouth, holding her folds open with one hand as he eased the index finger of the other into her tight entrance.

Yes. Yes. Fill me. I feel so empty.

Adding a second finger, he groaned against her pussy, "Jesus, Maddie. You're so fucking tight and so damn hot."

It had been years, and she was tight, but the stretching felt so incredibly good. She lifted her hips, begging for more. "Make me come. Please." Her body was ready to spontaneously combust and she was already misted with perspiration, every cell in her body crying out for release.

She gripped his head, pulling him tighter against her pussy, needing friction, begging for release.

His tongue moved over her clit and he began to devour. He flicked and laved, swallowing her cream with a hungry groan, his fingers fucking her in a wild, abandoned rhythm as he stimulated her clit with his tongue and gentle nips of his mouth.

"Sam. Oh, God. Yes," she hissed, her body clenching, her release rushing up to hit her full force. The walls of her channel clenched tightly around his fingers, as her whole body pulsated and trembled with the powerful climax.

Her hands clenched and released in his hair, shuddering as the silken strands fell over her fingers.

Incredible.

Every one of her senses felt hypersensitive. Panting, she came down slowly as Sam continued to lap at every drop of her orgasm greedily, extending her pleasure until it was almost unbearable.

As he came to his knees, she could see every vein in his cock engorged, and his face was fierce, so carnal that her channel spasmed with the desire to have him inside her.

Wanting to pleasure him as he had pleasured her, she reached for his massive member, wanting to feel the silky texture of it under her fingers. She sat up, making contact with her fingers, touching the moist, bulbous head with a sigh.

"No. Maddie, don't." Sam grabbed her wrist so tightly that it startled her. Peering up at his face, his expression stopped her from lowering her mouth to him. He looked panicked and anxious. The look only lasted a few heartbeats and then it was gone, followed by an expression of remorse.

Loosening his hold on her wrist, he lowered his fiery body to hers. "I'm sorry. Sometimes I just don't like to be…touched." His voice was frustrated.

She pulled her wrist from his hand and wrapped her arms around his neck. "Can I touch you like this?" She wrapped her legs around his waist and pressed her breasts to his chest. She stroked her fingers over the rippling muscles of his back, down to his waist, and back up again.

"Oh, fuck yeah. Touch me just like that," he groaned, his voice tortured.

"I need you, Sam."

"I need you, too, Sunshine. Now." He reached down and positioned himself at her snug entrance. "You're so fucking tight. I don't want to hurt you." He eased the tip into her, and she heard him grunt, his body already damp with the strain of holding back.

"Just fuck me, Sam. Now. Don't go easy or gentle. I need you."
She wanted him thrusting, filling her over and over. She didn't give
a damn if it was a tight fit; she just needed his cock inside her now.

He propelled himself inside her with a forceful thrust, burying
himself in her tight cavern. Maddie moaned, stretched to her max-
imum, full of Sam. At that moment, nothing else existed in the
outside world. There was only her hunger for the man taking her,
reclaiming her, mastering her body.

"I've dreamed of this, Maddie. So many times," he choked out
as he pulled out and drove himself home again. "It was never this
good in my dreams."

"Mine either," she panted, her legs wrapping tighter around his
hips, begging for more. "Fuck me, Sam. Make those dreams finally
be real."

Everything was raw and carnal, needy and desperate. Sam pummeled her with his cock, driving deeply, grasping her ass to bring
them together again and again. The air was heavy around them, and
their damp bodies slid together in an erotic glide as they reached
for their peak.

"Come for me, Sunshine. Come for me. I want to watch you this
time."

His words sent her spinning over the edge, her climax roaring
through her body like a violent storm. Holding on to Sam for dear
life, her nails digging into his back, she exploded, crying out as her
muscles spasmed, her release flooding over Sam's cock, bathing it
with lush heat.

Her back arched, her breasts abraded by the fine hairs on his chest,
making her body tremble. Throwing her head back, she screamed his
name as the whole world flew apart; the only thing of any substance
being the man she was clinging to, his muscular bulk preventing
her from whirling into space.

Sam followed her into release with an agonized groan, his warmth
flooding her womb as his body shuddered over hers.

"Fuck. Holy fuck." He collapsed on top of her, his chest heaving,
his breathing ragged. "Shit. I'll crush you." He rolled to his back

beside her, pulling her against his side, wrapping his arms around her.

They were silent as their heartbeats slowed and their bodies came down from their orgasmic high. Maddie rested her head on his chest, her body more sated and content than it had ever been.

"We didn't use a condom," she finally mentioned in a remorseful voice.

"I gave you my medical records," he said, his voice slightly hoarse.

She hadn't read them yet, but it wasn't diseases she was worried about. He wouldn't have given her his medical records to clear himself if everything wasn't negative. "I didn't give you mine," she replied with a sigh.

"Then I guess we share whatever you have. If it's fatal, I'll die with you," he answered, completely seriously. "I can't be without you anymore, Maddie. It's too fucking painful."

She had to swallow the lump in her throat. She felt the same way. Living without Sam had been like living in the dark, waiting for daylight to come. "I'm clean. But I'm not on birth control. It's not a likely time of month, but it was still careless. I'm a freaking doctor, for goodness' sake!"

"You're marrying me, anyway," he rumbled, rolling to trap her body beneath his. "You are marrying me, Maddie." It wasn't a question. It was a demand.

She smiled, eyeing her alpha male above her, so damn masculine in his dominance. "I said we'd discuss it later."

"It is later. And you're mine," he stated possessively.

"We'll see," she murmured, pulling him down for a tender kiss that quickly grew passionate. Kissing Sam was like putting a flame to gasoline, the ignition almost immediate and white-hot.

"Are you trying to change the subject?" Sam demanded when he came up for air.

"No. Not really. I was just hoping to make up for lost time," she told him seductively, teasingly.

"I thought you didn't like sex," he reminded her in a sultry voice.

"I'm starting to change my opinion." She ran the sole of her foot along his calf playfully.

"I think I need to work on you doing a total three-sixty," he answered in a husky voice.

"Are you always able to do anything you set your mind to?" She gave him a torrid look.

"Damn right I can," he said aggressively, burying his fingers in her fiery, disheveled mane of hair.

As he proceeded to master her with just one kiss, Maddie was fairly certain that he was correct.

Chapter 8

"Sam proposed to you?" Kara squealed in delight as she hugged Maddie, her packing forgotten.

Maddie hugged her friend in return. "Um…I wouldn't say it was exactly a proposal. It was more like an ultimatum."

Kara laughed lightly, sitting on the bed beside her suitcase, staring up at Maddie. "Figures. He's a Hudson male. I think world domination is in their genes, especially Sam's, and they both have a severe overload of protective instinct with the women they love."

Maddie shared a knowing smile with Kara. After she and Sam had snuck back into the house and up the back stairs, they had separated, Sam explaining that he had some business with Simon before he and Kara left on their honeymoon. Maddie had quickly showered and come to say goodbye to Kara, and had promptly told her everything, desperately needing to talk to her friend about Sam. Kara was probably one of the few people who understood the Hudson men.

"He never said he loves me. And it's more like a business proposition than a marriage," Maddie replied, her heart sinking. The minute they had left the dock, she had felt Sam drawing away, the closeness they had found in each other's arms receding.

"Maddie, it's always been pretty obvious that you and Sam had something going, something that never ended for either of you. I can verify that the story about him helping the FBI is true. Simon told me about Sam helping to break up the organization. Simon's always admired Sam for it. But they did have to be protected for quite a while. I have no doubt that everything Sam said is true," Kara said softly, thoughtfully. "For all his faults, Sam's a good man. What are you going to do?"

"I don't know," Maddie answered her honestly. "He's pushing and I need time. Hell, we don't even know each other anymore. Our relationship was years ago. We were barely adults. So much has happened since then. We've both changed."

"Uh…I can tell you from personal experience that patience isn't exactly a Hudson virtue," Kara snickered.

Maddie rolled her eyes. "I discovered that a long time ago." She waved her hand at the open suitcase. "Speaking of which, you better get packing, girlfriend."

Kara stood, her eyes soft and warm as she spoke. "Maddie, I doubt that either Sam or Simon could have survived the childhood they had without some collateral damage. Don't listen to Sam's bluster; look into his heart."

"I'm not sure he'll let me in," Maddie admitted. "I don't really understand any of this. Everything is happening so fast."

Kara folded a pair of jeans and dropped them into the suitcase. "I don't think so. I don't think Sam ever got over you. For him, it never ended."

"I don't think I did either," Maddie whispered, knowing what she said was true. Sam may have changed over the years, but he was still…Sam. She had been able to resist him when she thought he had cheated on her, when she had thought she had loved a man who had never existed. Now that she knew he had been trying to protect her, that he had wanted her, stopping herself from falling back into his spider web of sweltering heat and desperate need was nearly impossible.

"Give him a chance. Sam's always been restless, unhappy. He covers it up well, but he's miserable," Kara remarked, her voice pleading. "I want both of you to be happy."

Maddie sighed. "I'll try to slow things down so we can get to know each other again."

Kara snorted. "Good luck with that. When a Hudson male decides he wants, he takes, and Lord help the woman if she protests."

"You learned to manage Simon," Maddie reminded her friend teasingly.

"He just lets me think I'm managing him. I'm really not. He pacifies me, but he's really quite devious," Kara replied, her voice adoring.

"Do you ever get used to it? Someone wanting you that much?" Maddie asked contemplatively.

"Oh yeah. It's completely addictive. What woman doesn't want to know that she's the center of her man's world?" Kara responded dreamily. "I went from being alone to being completely ecstatic. I'll take Simon's obsession any day compared to a man who doesn't give a shit. He loves me and his obsession makes me feel safe, protected, wanted. If some of the things he does are a little over the top, I don't care. It's actually pretty hot. All that matters is how much we love each other."

Maddie shuddered, knowing she felt the same way. Sam's dominant, overprotective attitude was completely hot. She had pretty much felt unwanted her entire life, and Sam's desperation for her made her totally insane, wanting him in the same unguarded manner. "Maybe that's what bothers me. I could get addicted to him so easily."

Kara laughed and winked as she closed her suitcase. "Then get addicted. Wallow in it. I doubt he's going to stop. Stubbornness is another Hudson trait. Once they decide they want, they don't stop even after they get it."

Maddie didn't tell Kara she had already had a taste of that seductive wanting. "I'm going to miss you." She hugged Kara tightly. "Have fun."

Simon and Kara were going on a three-week tour of the UK and Europe for their honeymoon, and Maddie was happy for Kara. Her friend hadn't had a very easy life and Kara deserved the best.

"I'll call you," Kara said emphatically as she hugged Maddie back. "I won't be able to stand this cliffhanger. I'll need to know what's happening."

"I think I'll have to figure out what's happening myself before I can tell you anything," Maddie said laughingly as she released her friend.

Kara put her hands on her hips, shooting Maddie a disapproving look. "At least take him up on funding the clinic. You know you want to."

Unfortunately, Maddie knew she wanted to take Sam up on the entire deal. She just wasn't sure her heart would survive it.

"If you want her, marry her."

Sam stared at his brother, Simon, wishing it were just that easy. "I am marrying her. I already told her that."

"Uh…did you actually ask her?" Simon inquired uneasily.

"Nope. I told her she was marrying me. She's had years to find somebody else and she hasn't. She's getting me. At least I won't treat her like shit and I can give her everything she wants. She'll get over the fact that she hates me…eventually." *I hope.*

When Sam had parted from Maddie upstairs, he had come down to the library and spilled everything to Simon, needing a male opinion.

"Shit. At least I asked Kara to marry me. I wasn't planning to let her refuse, but at least I did ask," Simon grumbled, shooting his older brother a troubled stare.

"I told her I wanted her to marry me. Same damn thing," Sam answered, his voice irritable.

"Uh…not exactly, bro," Simon answered. "I don't think Maddie's the type of woman who wants to be told what to do. She's kind of like Kara in that way. You have to let Maddie think she's managing things once in a while."

"Why?" Sam demanded, shooting his brother a disgusted look. "If I do that, she could bolt. I'm not willing to let her get away this time. She's marrying me."

Simon nodded emphatically. "Right. Well, in that case, you don't have a choice. You'll just have to make her marry you."

"Oh, good grief. Am I really hearing my two sons discussing marriage as though they were arranging something in the Stone Age? Samuel Hudson, you are going to court that woman appropriately and then politely ask her to marry you." Their mother, Helen Hudson, strode into the room, shooting Sam a harsh, admonishing look.

Oh, shit. I hate that look. Makes me feel like a five-year-old.

Sam shot his mother a charming smile, even though he knew it wouldn't work. Mom had been on to him forever. "We were just discussing possible options, Mom."

Helen walked over to him and craned her neck to look up into his eyes. Strange, but even though his mother had to look up at him now, that knowing glance still made him want to squirm like a naughty child.

"You treat that woman right or you'll lose your chance," she warned him sternly. "I saw the way you were with her today. You need her."

Sam couldn't argue with that statement. He definitely needed Maddie. The question was…how to get her where he wanted her.

Simon was sitting behind the desk, his mother's back to him, and Sam saw him smirking.

"And don't be sassy, Simon. You married a wonderful woman today. You need to treat her right," Helen admonished, without even turning around, making Simon sit up in his chair and wipe the smile from his face.

Sam looked at his mother affectionately. The woman really did have eyes in the back of her head.

"I treat Kara like a princess," Simon objected, slouching back in the office chair.

"You better continue to do it," his mother answered.

Helen was still dressed for the wedding, looking stunning in a navy blue dress with matching pumps. Her blonde hair was still nicely coiffed and she didn't look in the least bit wilted from the long day she had put in helping from sunrise until just this moment. Even though Sam had told her to go home, she had stayed to oversee the clean-up.

Wish I would have remembered she was still here. I would have closed the door.

Folding her arms in front of her impatiently, Helen asked sharply, "Did I…or did I not hear you say you were going to *make* that girl marry you, Samuel?"

Dammit. He was really in trouble if she was calling him Samuel.

"She's going to marry me," he told his mother stubbornly.

"She's educated, she's smart, and she's beautiful. Stop treating her like you have dominant caveman genes and maybe you'll succeed. You can't just club the woman over the head and drag her away to your cave. She deserves your respect," Helen admonished him.

"I do respect her. I wouldn't want to marry her if I didn't," Sam argued.

"Then treat her well and stop acting like an ass," Helen retorted. "I'd like to see you as happy as Simon is, Sam," she finished in a wistful voice. She lifted her palm to cup his cheek. "You both deserve to be happy."

Sam bent and bussed his mother's cheek. Helen Hudson hadn't had an easy life, and she had given both he and Simon as much as she possibly could when she was raising them, including her love. He knew she wanted him to be happy.

"Are we ready?" Kara strode into the room, dressed to travel in jeans, a trendy sweater, and ankle boots, with Maddie following behind her.

Simon jumped out of the chair so fast he nearly tipped it over. "Yeah. I'm ready, sweetheart. Let's go."

Sam nearly burst into laughter at Simon's eagerness. He knew his brother was not only ready to start his honeymoon, but impatient to get away from Mom when she was in one of her rare lecturing moods.

Maddie stood beside Kara, having showered and changed into jeans and another breast-hugging shirt. The three women locked arms and headed toward the door, hugging and kissing like they would never see each other again. Kara had been a friend of his mother's for years, and Maddie had become very friendly with Mom over the last year.

Sam started after them, ready to see *everybody* out. He wanted to be alone with Maddie.

Simon snagged his arm, uttering in a low voice, "I say stick with the plan. Use the club if you need to."

Sam nodded, mesmerized by Maddie's gently swaying hips as she walked with Kara and his mom to the door.

Mine.

Feral possessiveness slammed him in the gut as he watched his woman smile at his mom and Kara.

He turned his head to see Simon staring at Kara in exactly the same way.

Simon turned to Sam and the brothers' eyes locked, exchanging an intense look of understanding and agreement before they both nodded emphatically at the same time.

He'd give Maddie as much time as he could, but eventually he'd give in and use the caveman tactics. He wouldn't be able to help himself. He needed her so damn much, even if he didn't deserve her.

Thinking about his reaction when she'd attempted to touch his cock, he frowned. He should have at least tried to explain. But that was a part of his past he didn't want to remember, didn't want to explain, even to Maddie. Especially to Maddie. He didn't want to see the look of revulsion when he told her, when she realized just how contaminated he was by his past. He'd done what he'd needed to do to protect his brother. Still, it had tainted him, and Maddie might be a doctor, but she was still so incredibly sweet. That part of his life was in the past and he wanted it to stay there.

But I rejected her, pushed her away.

Because he had needed to do it. Thinking about it just made him feel less worthy of a woman like Maddie. She didn't need to be polluted by his bullshit.

I wanted her touch. I wanted to feel her mouth on me.

His reaction had been instinctive, an aversion that he'd had since he was a child. Since there were certain things he didn't want sexually, he'd made an art out of pleasuring a woman. And Maddie *had* been pleasured. She had climaxed so beautifully, so erotically. Just thinking about it nearly made him groan aloud as he raked his hand through his hair in frustration. Every sexual experience he had ever had paled beside that incredible encounter with Maddie, his every sexual fantasy come to life.

Trying to block his past, trying not to remember how very fucked up he still was, he went to join the others.

Chapter 9

It was several days before Maddie actually read Sam's medical records. Strangely, he hadn't made love to her again at his house. They'd gone to bed after Kara, Simon, and Helen had left, exhausted from the events of the wedding. She had slept in his enormous bed, actually longing for him to touch her, but he hadn't. Somehow, he seemed distant, not at all as they had been during their incredible experience out on the dock. He remained aloof the next day. They had spent a lazy morning and afternoon watching movies in his home theater, and then she had needed to get back home to take care of some personal business before returning to work.

She had agreed to his business proposition of taking over the clinic as a charitable entity, and she had given the hospital her notice. Sam had stubbornly insisted on her not going back to work at the clinic until she was ready to start full-time. He was keeping paid staff there until she could do so. She hadn't liked it, but she had agreed. If working full-time at the clinic meant she had to wait a few weeks to go back, she'd do it.

He hadn't mentioned marriage again after they had hammered out an agreement for the clinic. She'd left his house with a brief goodbye and plans to improve the clinic, and he had told her he would call her.

It had been three days, and she still hadn't heard from him. Now, disquiet was beginning to set in, and Maddie's brain was working overtime.

Something's not right. His reaction to me when I touched him was as if...

She flipped open the manila folder, taking a sip of her wine as she relaxed in a comfortable pair of old pajamas on her couch. Not even sure why she was reading the file, she turned the pages, finding his recent physical and his negative results for all sexual diseases and blood work. It wasn't exactly a shocker that he was in superb physical condition after seeing his body in the raw, up close and personal, an incredible specimen of male perfection.

Trying not to think about *that*, she kept turning the pages, seeing very little except a few incidents of viruses over the last ten or twelve years, but nothing significant.

Maddie knew she had seen enough to know that Sam was medically doing fine, but curiosity made her flip to the thick file in the back of his medical documents, wondering what had happened to accumulate so many old records.

Her eyes grew wide as she realized they were all psychological records, documentation of visits with a psychologist.

Victim of sexual abuse...forceful anal penetration resulting in rectal bleeding...fondling of the genitals...occurring from age eleven to age twelve.

Maddie tore her eyes away from the records with a horrified gasp. Putting a hand to her racing heart, she tried to calm her frenzied breathing.

Dear God, no! It had to be wrong. Not Sam. Please, not Sam.

She downed her wine in a couple of gulps and put the file on the couch to fetch another glass, her thoughts racing.

She returned with a very full wine glass, her body shaking as she sat down again. As a physician, Maddie had seen plenty of rape and molestation cases. Every one of them was horrifying, but she just couldn't seem to wrap her mind around the fact that Sam had suffered in that way.

Sometimes, I just don't like to be...touched.

Maddie shuddered, remembering his deep baritone saying those words, the brief look of fear in his eyes as he said them. She had known something was wrong, that it was an instinctive reaction. Somewhere deep in her mind alarm bells had sounded even then, knowing it was the reaction of a man who had somehow been hurt.

"Shit. I wouldn't want to be touched there either if someone had violated me," she whispered to herself.

Setting her wine on the coffee table, she lifted the file again. He had started therapy and stayed with it for three years. Skipping the account of all of the graphic incidents, she read the psychologist's notes that had started several years after her relationship with Sam and that had continued for three years after the first date of therapy. Tears poured from her eyes as she read, an occasional sob escaping as she read the accounts of how Sam had struggled to deal with the problems arising from the molestation. He had been so damn brave, probably much braver than she would have been in his situation. Sam had initiated the therapy himself, wanting to get over some of the symptoms he was having that were similar to PTSD. And he had healed. There were some things that would always take work and patience, but he had tried to heal much of the trauma.

Maybe she should feel guilty for reading his history, but she didn't. Sam still had a few things he needed to work on, and she couldn't help him if he didn't talk to her. No doubt he wanted to leave it in the past, but there were some things that apparently still haunted him, things that would only be overcome by learning to trust.

Maddie knew Sam hadn't meant for her to see these records. He had obviously asked somebody for his medical records and they had provided them. Everything. Including his visits for therapy.

Wiping her saturated face with the sleeve of her pajamas, she finished her glass of wine and flipped to the beginning of the psychological evaluation, not ready to read about the actual incidents, but compelled to do so. She tried to look at it clinically, as a medical doctor reading a patient history, but it didn't work. She sobbed as she read, her heart tearing to pieces with every incident, unable to picture anything but her beloved Sam, as an eleven-year-old boy, being hurt by men that got off by torturing him.

She had barely finished reading when the overwhelming nausea struck, making her run to the bathroom, still keening for Sam's pain. As a physician, Dr. Madeline Reynolds had a will of steel and a cast-iron stomach. But as a woman, Maddie heaved until she was lightheaded and dizzy, totally forgetting she was a physician, reacting only as a woman who loved.

The next evening, Maddie stopped at the clinic after work, and felt completely out of sorts. The fill-in young male physician, Dr. Turner, seemed to have everything under control with the help of a young, blonde nurse who seemed to idolize the handsome doctor. Feeling bereft and bored, she headed for the restaurant where she had agreed to meet Max Hamilton. She had two days off, and nothing planned.

She sighed, unused to not being busy every minute of every day. It felt good to actually have some free time, but the days were lonely when she had nothing to occupy herself. Her only plans were dinner this evening and probably two days of cleaning her house, a job that she only did sporadically when she had the time. It could use a heavy cleaning and she had nothing else planned.

She let out a deep breath as she turned in to the restaurant, acknowledging that she missed Sam. But she would let him contact her when he was ready. Strangely, she had no doubt that he would.

The restaurant was a nice one, a place known for steak and seafood. She'd never been here, but she was glad she had worn a dress and heels. The weather was miserable, windy and stormy, the temperatures below normal. She put her hands in her pockets as she hustled to the door, shivering as she went through the entrance.

"Dr. Reynolds?" The hostess greeted her immediately.

Surprised, and grateful for the warmth of the interior, she answered, "Yes?"

"Your party is here. I'll take you to your table." The tall brunette waited for Maddie to come up behind her and led her through the sophisticated restaurant to a quiet table in the corner. The décor was quietly elegant, finished mostly in black and white with modern but tasteful prints, one wall constructed entirely of glass to overlook the water.

Max Hamilton rose as Maddie arrived at the table, a genuine smile on his lips as he said, "Hi, Maddie. I'm so glad you could make it."

He was suave and elegant in a tan suit and navy and tan matching tie, every inch of him exuding power and control, but she had never sensed any harmful intentions behind his smile, and she still didn't.

He seated her before returning to his own chair. "What would you like to drink?" he asked, summoning a waiter, and ordering a Scotch on the rocks for himself.

Shrugging out of her coat, she answered, "Just a glass of wine. Anything that isn't extremely dry is fine."

Max placed an order for a glass of white Zinfandel as she accepted a menu from the waiter.

He openly stared at her after the waiter left, his expression unreadable. Maddie looked at him with open fascination. What was it about this man that drew her, made her want to hug him until he didn't feel so alone anymore? Loneliness and sorrow seemed to hang over him like a dark cloud, even though she'd mostly seen him smiling. She could sense both emotions, subliminal, yet heartbreaking.

Tearing her eyes away from his face, she picked up her menu. "What's good? I've never been here before."

He grinned. "Everything. It just depends on what you'd like."

"I'm not exactly a picky eater," she answered in a self-mocking tone.

Their drinks arrived and they ordered. Max asked her a million questions while they sipped their drinks and during dinner, his interest flattering. By the time they had their dessert, they were talking like old friends.

"So tell me how you know Simon and Sam?" she asked curiously before taking a bite of her incredible-looking chocolate mousse.

"We've joined forces in ventures together for years. Sam has a knack for picking all the right ones. I just invest," he answered, placing his spoon on his plate, his dessert finished.

"That's not true," she retorted, naming some prominent ventures that had been his initial idea.

He looked startled. "I guess you really pay attention to the financial news. Probably watching Sam," he guessed...correctly.

Maddie hated to admit that she'd followed Hudson and its financial achievements for years.

Max put up a hand. "I'm not offended. Don't worry. It's obvious you and Sam have something going on. I like Sam. I'm not even thinking of stepping on his toes. I just want to be...friends." His voice hesitated on the last word.

Maddie examined his expression. He seemed sincere, but she suspected that there was something else he wanted. Her best guess is that what he really wanted was companionship, something to take away the loneliness she could feel radiating from his soul, a sense of loneliness so profound that it was nearly tangible.

"Where are your parents, family?" she asked, trying to decipher why this man seemed so solitary.

"I was an only child. And my parents died in a car accident ten years ago," he answered quietly.

He's alone. Completely alone. A kindred soul. Maddie knew exactly how that felt, and her heart bled for him. She almost wished she hadn't asked.

He smiled at her, a warm smile that made his handsome face even more attractive. "I had great parents. I was lucky, even though I lost them way too soon."

She finished her dessert as she listened to him reminisce about memories of his parents, funny stories in happier times. Obviously, he had dealt with that loss. It had to be the more recent loss of his wife that really haunted him.

"You know Sam doesn't really sleep around, don't you?" Max asked her after he had paused in his family stories to down the rest of his Scotch.

Maddie nearly choked on her wine. "Excuse me?" she queried, not sure if she had understood what Max was asking.

Max shrugged. "I'm just saying…the stories about Sam for the most part aren't true. He might take some of his female friends to parties, but he doesn't sleep with them like people think he does. He's gotten a bad reputation that he really doesn't deserve," he finished casually, but his eyes were intense.

"And how would you know that it isn't true?" she questioned, wondering where this whole conversation was headed.

"Sam and I have known each other a long time. We go to a lot of the same functions, socialize in the same circles. Most of the time we go together. When my wife was alive, we would go with Sam and his female date for the evening. We'd all go out for drinks together usually, but we dropped Sam's date off first, and then Sam. At home. Alone." He heaved a deep breath before continuing, "Now that my wife is gone, Sam and I drop his date first and then go hang out together. But we both leave alone." His brows drew together as he stared at her. "Understand?"

Maddie smiled slightly. "So you're trying to tell me that he isn't the man-whore he's made out to be by the press?"

"I'm not saying he's an angel, but he's not the man most people think he is. I just happen to know about his sleeping arrangements because we go to functions together, though Simon usually avoids them whenever possible, which is most of the time." Max pulled out his credit card and speared it into the leather enclosed bill that had been brought discreetly to the table by the waiter. He dropped it onto the edge of the table and looked her directly in the eye. "I've only met one of his lovers, and she was a petite redhead, completely unlike the female friends he takes to charity events and other functions, and that was a long time ago. Why do you think that might be?"

I haven't been with a woman in months. I fucking couldn't. Before that I only slept with women who had red hair, curvy bodies and who didn't mind that I called out your name when I came. Women who only wanted money or material things because I had nothing else to give them.

Oh, God. Sam *had* been telling the truth. Tearing her eyes away from Max, she stared at the wall behind him. "Why? He could pick almost any single woman in the world and she would drop at his feet to be with him. Why?"

Max shrugged. "Being wealthy can be a curse as much as a blessing at times. Having money can make a man wonder if the woman really wants him, or just the money and power. Unfortunately, in our circles, most women care more about the money than the man," he said, his tone slightly bitter. "Don't get me wrong, Sam and I both like the money and the power; we thrive on it. But it does have its disadvantages in the relationship department."

"But don't most men like having women fall all over them?" she asked curiously, her gaze returning to his face.

"It depends on the man, I guess. It gets pretty old and pretty unattractive after a while. And damn lonely."

"Why are you telling me this, Max?" Maddie really wanted to know. "Are you matchmaking?"

Max barked out a startled laugh. "Hell no. It would actually be to my advantage if I didn't tell you. I wouldn't mind monopolizing your time and I have a feeling that Sam is going to try to kill me for taking you to dinner. He isn't exactly subtle about his interest."

"Well…he won't hear about it from me." Maddie put two fingers to her mouth and mimicked zipping her lips.

Max's lips turned up in a knowing smile. "No…but he'll hear it from *them*." He nodded subtly at a table across the room where two bulky men, looking uncomfortably out of place, stared blatantly at the two of them.

"Does Sam know them?" she asked, confused.

"Yeah. Pretty well. They work for him. Part of his security team," Max answered wryly. "I've seen them before. They're obviously your tail."

"He's spying on me?" she answered, outraged that Sam would have her followed.

Max reached his hand across the table and grabbed her arm before she could rise. "Maddie…don't. They aren't spies. They're protection.

He's a high-profile guy who's been connected to you romantically. That makes you a possible target. Believe me, I'd do the same if I was seriously seeing someone. Sam's made plenty of enemies. Powerful enemies. That's one of the reasons he's never seen with a woman showing any open affection. But the picture of Sam carrying you around like a caveman at the wedding was everywhere. And he obviously plans to take it even further in the future. He wants you safe." He held her hand across the table, keeping her seated, his voice calming. "Actually, I can't believe he hasn't called yet. He is going to know what you're doing most of the time. He's probably a little slow because he's sick."

Maddie wasn't sure how she felt about Sam knowing her every move. It was a little uncomfortable. Yeah, she understood his protective streak, but having someone on her tail constantly was disconcerting. "Did you say he was sick?" she asked, not sure if she had heard Max properly.

"Flu. He's got it bad." Max shook his head, looking concerned for his friend. "He's been working from home. Not available. I talked to his assistant, David."

"Damn it. I wondered why he hasn't called me. Stubborn man," she said, squeezing Max's hand while she stood up. "I need to go see if he's okay."

Max chuckled as he released her hand and stood. "Wait. I'll walk you out." He pulled a gold pen from his pocket and signed the credit card receipt that the waiter had dropped on their table and pocketed his card. "Maddie, he probably doesn't want you to get sick."

Maddie shoved her arms into the jacket that Max was politely holding out for her. She buttoned the jacket and propped her hands on her hips. "I'm a damn doctor. I got my flu shot. I'm exposed to the flu every day."

Max held out his arm to her and she took it. "I can assure you that he isn't thinking rationally. His only thought is protecting you."

"Great. And who's protecting him?" she replied, irritated.

"I doubt anyone has ever thought he needed it," Max answered thoughtfully.

"He does, dammit. He doesn't need to always be the protector," she answered stubbornly, wishing someone had been there to protect him when he was younger. "Everyone needs support sometimes."

Max walked her to her car before he answered in a low, emotional voice, "You know, I do believe you're right. Take care of him, Maddie."

Giving in to her compulsion to soothe Max, she hugged him. He wrapped his arms around her and squeezed her back, both of them staying in that position for a moment as some sort of mysterious connection was cemented between them.

"I'll call you." Max let go of her reluctantly and opened her car door.

"Talk to you soon," she answered, her soul still slightly unsettled from the way she was drawn to Max's suffering.

"Don't let Sam boss you around," Max said laughingly as Maddie settled herself in the car.

She chortled. "Not happening or I'll find a reason he suddenly needs a shot in the ass," she assured Max. Sam was going to listen to her and he was going to get well.

She heard Max's delighted laugh as he closed her car door. She exited the parking lot and headed straight toward Sam's house, trying not to notice his security trailing behind her.

Chapter 10

S am groaned as he rolled over in bed and pulled the pillow over his head, feeling so damn miserable that he wished he could just sleep until he felt recovered. Sweat rolled off his body in tiny ringlets that were slowly saturating his sheets, and he shivered from the damp linens beneath him.

"Fuck!" He muttered the curse, but not too loud. If he made any sudden movements, those little men in his head with the hammers would start banging away again.

There wasn't a part of his body that didn't ache and his ribs were screaming in protest from his nearly-constant cough.

He heard a ruckus coming from downstairs, but he ignored it. Whatever it was, his security would handle it. It was what he paid them to do. Right now, he just wanted to be alone in his misery.

"I don't care if he isn't seeing anyone. He's seeing me. I'm his doctor."

Maddie. Shit.

Sam struggled to sit up, but ended up flat on his back again as dizziness assaulted him, making the whole room spin.

I hate this shit. I'm so fucking weak. And if there was one thing Sam hated, it was feeling helpless.

His door burst open and he cracked one eye open to see the most beautiful sight in the world.

Maddie.

He scowled as he saw two security agents holding her by the arms on both sides. "Get your fucking hands off her. And don't ever touch her again." His voice was hoarse, but he got his point across.

The guards released her like she was a hot coal. "Sorry, Mr. Hudson. She broke away at the door and we couldn't catch her. You said you weren't to be disturbed."

"She's the exception. Always," he grunted. "Now leave."

The guards left, leaving Maddie standing by the door. She closed the door and came to the side of the bed, one hand on her hip. She placed a cool hand on his forehead gently, smoothing the damp hair from his face. "What in the hell are you doing to yourself? You're burning up. Are you taking anything?"

"Don't need pills. I'll get over it," he croaked, watching her in curious fascination.

She marched into the master bathroom, and Sam could hear her rifling through the cabinets. "What the hell! Don't you have anything except condoms in here?"

Sam knew it was a rhetorical question, but as she came back out looking like a wild-eyed, furious goddess, he answered, "No. I don't take pills. Never need them."

She picked up his cell phone from the bedside table and started scanning his numbers, punching one with a vengeance. After she verified that she had Sam's personal assistant on the line, she started rattling off orders like a drill sergeant. She hung up the phone with an angry punch to the *off* button and called another number, a pharmacy from what he could gather by the conversation. She finished, slamming his smartphone back onto the bedside table with enough force to make him wince.

"You need clean sheets and fluids. Can you manage to get in the shower if I help you?" she asked, her voice demanding.

Like his tiny little woman was going to hold his weight? He smirked. "You know, this bossy doctor thing is pretty hot. Will you scrub my back?"

"If necessary," she snipped back at him as she started stripping the sheets from his sweat-ridden body.

Not wanting her to see his weakness, Sam made a superhuman effort to sit up. He made it, but he swayed as he got to his feet and started coughing so hard he couldn't stop. She propped him up with her body, which was surprisingly strong. "For a man who's supposedly a complete genius, you're an idiot when it comes to taking care of yourself," she commented, sounding like a cat that was spitting mad.

Holy hell, she was completely hot when she was in a take-charge mood. "You need to go. I didn't want you to know. You might get sick." His gut rolled at the thought of Maddie feeling as miserable as he did right now.

"I'm exposed to this every day, Sam. Why didn't you call me earlier?" she asked, exasperated. "You have tons of people at your beck and call. You needed help."

"Don't ask for help. I help other people," he grumbled as he walked like a drunk toward the bathroom. Honestly, it had never occurred to him to ask anybody for anything. He hated being vulnerable and preferred to wait until he had control again.

She stripped off his boxers, the only item of clothing on his body, and turned on the shower. "Will you be okay while I go find some fresh sheets and change the bed?"

"Yeah," he said, squawking as the lukewarm water hit his body.

"Don't make it any hotter. You're already too feverish," she warned him, giving him a commanding look.

Really, the woman was completely sexy in her doctor mode. A feisty redheaded virago who he wished he could tame right about now. Unfortunately, he wasn't in any position to drag her into the cubicle and take her against the shower stall. Damn...he wished he was. He'd like nothing better than to tap all of that passion she had right now. "Where were you?" he asked, wondering why she was dressed in a soft gray angora sweater dress, a color that just made her hair look more fiery and hugged the curves of her body like a lover. It probably wasn't made to be sexy, but on her, it definitely was.

"I was out for dinner before I came here." She pulled off her heels as she left the bathroom, leaving the door open.

With who?

He wanted to know, but Maddie had left like her ass was on fire. He let the water pour onto his body, rinsing the perspiration from his skin. He eyed the water temperature, tempted to ignore her and make it hotter, but his woman was likely to kick his ass right now. Problem was, she probably could. He smiled as he leaned into the water, letting it cleanse him. He wanted to really wash, but he was drained, using all of his energy just to stand under the water.

Maddie came back five minutes later. He watched, completely mesmerized, as she efficiently stripped every article of clothing from her body, leaving them in a heap on the floor. It wasn't a striptease, but then Maddie only needed to exist for him to get aroused, and watching her disrobe had his cock hard and ready for action. Unfortunately, the rest of his body wasn't.

Grabbing a washrag from the vanity, she entered the shower, shivering at the water temperature for a moment before getting to work. She lathered the washrag with soap and started running it over his skin, the linen gliding over him with her gentle touch.

She hesitated when she reached his groin and his whole body froze. He forcefully slammed down the instinct to stop her. This was Maddie, trying to help him. He was *not* pushing her away. He didn't want to push her away.

Maddie dropped the cloth, and Sam felt only her gentle hands on him as she moved over his groin and stroked his pulsating cock with her bare fingers. The sensation caused an initial startled reaction, but he kept his eyes on Maddie as she touched him, focusing only on her. Almost disappointed when she didn't linger there for long, he felt her hands move oh-so-tenderly over his ass. His butt cheeks tightened and he ground his teeth as she stroked between the globes of his ass, her fingers lightly going over his anus. He released a tormented growl, one part fear…but another part pleasure. Her touch was clinical, but achingly soft, enticingly delicate.

Crouching, she ran the soap over both of his legs. Then, she stood and washed his hair, her touch soothing as she gently massaged his scalp. After picking up the handheld showerhead attachment, she briskly rinsed both his hair and body, and turned off the shower. She dried herself roughly and hurriedly, but picked up another towel and sweetly caressed him with it, patting him dry. After quickly pulling a short, cotton nightgown over her head from the pile of clothes she had left on the vanity, she braced his body and brought him out to sit on the bed, helping him into a fresh pair of boxer briefs.

"Wow, David is efficient," she marveled as she picked up the juice from the bedside table and handed it to him. She shook pills from various bottles and held them to his mouth like she would do with a recalcitrant child. "I didn't think he'd get this stuff that fast."

"I pay him to be efficient," he grumbled. Sam was no fool. He opened his mouth, surprisingly obediently, and let her drop in the pills, downing them with a swig of the juice.

"Finish the drink. You need to keep hydrated. I just gave you something for your fever, congestion, cough, and pain. You'll probably sleep." She finger-combed his hair while she spoke, a concerned frown on her face.

Sam finished his glass of juice and Maddie took it from him. "Lay back and rest."

"Stay with me?" Sam asked, not able to help himself. He didn't give a shit if he sounded pathetic, his need for Maddie overcoming his pride.

"Of course I'm staying," she replied indignantly.

Sam smiled as she launched into a tirade that included stuff about "stubborn men" and other derogatory oaths about the male gender, and *him* in particular. His woman was angry with him for not taking care of himself. Somehow…the curses didn't bother him at all…they made his chest ache with tenderness for the only woman who had cared for him—cared about him—other than his mother.

He propped himself on a pillow, watching his fiery female stomp around the room, picking up clothes and straightening things he had discarded when he'd gotten ill and never picked up. She mumbled under her breath, but Sam had no doubt it was more of the same diatribe, so maybe he was glad he couldn't hear her. Instead, he drank in the sight of her, somehow feeling better just by watching her.

Showering had helped. He felt clean for the first time in days, and comfortable in fresh sheets. His headache was slowly easing and lethargy was claiming his body instead of misery.

His cock was as hard as a rock and it stiffened even more as she bent over, revealing her delectable ass. He gaped, unable to do anything else, leering at her bare backside as she bent to pick up her shoes.

She turned as she straightened, shooting him an admonishing look. "Are you staring at my butt? I need panties," she mumbled.

Oh, hell no you don't. He nearly groaned with disappointment as she ducked into the bathroom, obviously to find a pair of underwear in the new clothes he had bought her that she hadn't taken home with her.

After returning from the bathroom, she picked up a thermometer from the plethora of items that David had dropped off and popped it into his mouth. "Don't speak," she warned him, her brow arched.

He scowled and crossed his arms in front of him. Damned if he didn't want to pull the annoying thing out of his mouth just to be contrary.

Then she laughed, a light, amused sound that flowed over him like a healing balm. "You look like an ornery little boy," she chortled, putting her hand on his forehead.

The beep sounded and she removed the offending thermometer. "High," she mused. "But I think you're cooler than you were. I may have to wake you up tonight to give you more medication."

He frowned as she handed him more juice. The last thing he really wanted was to swallow. His throat felt like it had been worked over with sandpaper.

"Drink it. You need fluids," she answered as though she already knew what he was thinking.

He eyed her as he sipped the juice, watching the beautiful vixen shake medication from the bottles at the bedside, probably for later dosages. "Anybody ever tell you that you're a bossy doctor?" he asked dryly, handing the empty glass back to her.

Had anybody ever told her how hot she looked when she was pissed off?

Sitting the cup on the table, she folded her arms in front of her and gave him a chastising look. "Only my non-cooperative patients. If you weren't so stubborn, you'd think I was the sweetest doctor in existence," she answered in a pseudo sugary voice.

"Think you're sweet anyway," he admitted in a low, husky voice. "What happened to your head?" he questioned, scowling as he noticed a small bruise on her left temple that he hadn't noticed earlier.

"It's nothing. A little car accident. I just bumped my head." She slipped into the bed and pulled the covers over herself. She turned off the light at the bedside, plunging the room into darkness.

He lunged for her, pulling her back against him. *Christ, she feels good.* He pulled her back against his chest and buried his face in her wild tangle of silky hair. "There is no such thing as a little car accident. What the hell happened? When? Dammit. Nobody called me. Those agents are fucking fired," he growled, shuddering at the thought that Maddie had been involved in an accident and he hadn't known.

"You are not going to fire them. They dropped me off here because my car is probably totaled. I told them not to call you because I was on my way here anyway. It's not a big deal, Sam. I was on my way over and the weather sucks because it's been raining all day. Another car hydroplaned through a red light and hit me. I'm fine," she answered, sounding exasperated.

Sam's heart was beating so fast he couldn't catch his breath. *Fuck!* He clutched Maddie tighter, running his hands over her body. "What if you were injured worse than you thought?" he asked, panicked at the thought.

Maddie rolled to face him, putting her arms around his neck. "I wasn't. I'm fine, Sam. I'm worried about you. You're sick. Please sleep. They hit on the passenger side and I was just shaken up a little. I'm a doctor. I didn't hit hard enough to injure anything except my poor vehicle."

"You need a bigger vehicle, something safer. And newer," he answered, irritation and fear both present in his voice.

"Sleep," she insisted, cuddling against him.

Sam was groggy, probably from the medication, but he couldn't keep the images of Maddie's car being slammed, with her inside it, from haunting him. What if she had been seriously injured...or worse? Christ! Those images were going to torment him for a while. "Something bad could have happened," he finally answered gruffly.

"It didn't," Maddie said soothingly, placing her head on his shoulder and running her fingers through his hair gently, caressing the back of his head in gentle circles. "Please rest, Sam. I'm worried about you. You obviously have a bad case of the flu and you need to sleep."

His chest ached, but not from his illness. Her concerned, soft voice comforted him and he closed his eyes tightly, his emotional reaction to her protectiveness intense.

His maniacal concern for *her* safety and possessiveness he could handle. But having someone care for him was foreign, and he wasn't sure how to react to it. "I'm glad you're here, Sunshine," he muttered softly, rubbing his face in her hair.

"Call me next time, please," she requested sleepily.

"Nothing can happen to you, Maddie. I wouldn't live through it," he said in a husky voice.

Sam wondered how Max had even survived after losing his wife. The pain must have been excruciating if Max had felt anything like the obsessive need he had for the cuddly, redheaded miracle he held in his arms right now.

"I'm here, Sam," she whispered.

Thank God!

"You're marrying me," he rumbled, his eyes closing, drowsiness taking over his body.

She didn't answer. She just snuggled closer and sighed.

Sam didn't let her lack of response bother him. In fact, his lips curled up in a smile. It was progress. At least she hadn't argued and she hadn't said no.

With that positive thought in his head, he slept.

Chapter 11

Maddie stayed with Sam until he had completely recovered, spending her two days off getting him through the worst of the illness and then going to his house every night after work for the last several days to make sure he was taking care of himself properly. He was by far the worst patient she had ever had, and she had seen her share of horrible ones. Sam Hudson didn't like weakness of any kind, and obviously that included anything that hampered him physically.

At the moment, he looked like nothing but trouble, completely furious and irritated as he stared at her from his home office desk, leaning back in his chair, glowering.

Sam was hiding behind his façade again, and Maddie hated it. He'd shown some vulnerability during the time that he had been ill. But he was the bully again…back in full force. She could accept Sam's alpha male personality. In fact, there were times she adored it. However, *now* was not one of those moments, when he was uttering demands, without a compromise or reason for his actions.

"You're driving the new car. Period. End of discussion," he barked, as though she were one of his employees.

Maddie took a deep breath and blew it out. "Fine. If the discussion is over, I'm leaving. And you can take the car and shove it up your ass because I'm not driving it. You had no right to select a vehicle for me without asking and then demand I drive it. I'm not one of your damn employees."

Wishing she had never come to his house this evening, she tried to compose herself. All she'd wanted to do was make sure he was feeling okay, taking care of himself. He'd been a complete ass to her this evening, basically throwing her keys to a new metallic black Mercedes SUV that had probably cost more than most people's homes, and demanding that she drive it. It wasn't that she didn't love the vehicle. She actually did. Who wouldn't? Her problem was his attitude, his distance. He just commanded and expected her to jump to his demands. He was hiding again, worried that he had shown too much weakness, and was going way over the top to make up for the lapse during his illness. She understood what he was doing and his motivations for it. But dammit…it hurt.

"I know you're not one of my damn employees. If you were, you'd do what I tell you to do," he growled. "And if you walk out that door, I'll catch you."

Folding her arms in front of her, she glared at him. "Then what? How do you plan to force me to drive it?" she retorted, her voice starting to get shaky and emotional. "Damn it! You didn't even ask me if I liked it, if I wanted it. My opinion doesn't matter, as long as I do as you say. What the hell is wrong with you tonight?" A lone tear flowed down her cheek and she swiped at it impatiently. There was so much about Sam that she loved, but there were a few things she couldn't tolerate.

Bossy…okay. Occasionally.

Demanding in bed…hell yeah.

Protective…yep.

Distant and cold…hell no!

Sam stood and walked around the desk. "You're not leaving," he said huskily. "Why are you crying?"

Maddie sprinted for the door, not ready to answer that question.

Because I love you so much it hurts. Because I want to matter to you as much as you matter to me. Because when you shut me out and get cold, I get scared.

Pulling the door open frantically, desperate to escape, she felt Sam's body slam into her from behind, pushing the door closed, trapping her between his arms on both sides of her body.

She leaned her forehead against the door, tears escaping her eyes unchecked. "Please, just let me go."

"Tell me why you're crying. You don't like the car? I can take it back. Get something else, as long as it's safe. It's classy and it reminded me of you." He was panting, his breath warm against her ear.

Shit. He was softening, acting like *her* Sam again. *Here I go, up the roller coaster incline, wondering when I'm going to plummet again.*

"I can't handle this, Sam. Please." Her emotions were a jumbled mess, old baggage coming back to haunt her. She couldn't help it. Sam was so necessary to her happiness that it scared her when he became so icy and brittle.

"What did I do, Sunshine? Tell me." His voice was tender, emotional. "I'll fix it."

"When you're cold and distant, I get afraid that you don't want me anymore," she choked out emotionally. She hadn't meant to say it, but there it was. "I know it's old baggage, and I know I'm probably needier than most women when it comes to you, but I have to know that I'm important to you, that my opinions matter. That *I* matter." Even to herself, she sounded pathetic, but she couldn't help it. "When you distance yourself emotionally from me, acting cold, I get scared."

Sam wrapped his arms around Maddie's upper body, bringing her back against him, rocking her. "I'm sorry, sweetheart. So sorry," he murmured against her ear, rocking her back and forth against him. "I get scared, too. I'm afraid something will happen to you, and I won't be worth a shit if it does. Don't you understand how important you are to me?"

Maddie shook her head, her shoulders shaking from suppressed sobs of agony, temporarily haunted by her fears from the past.

Dammit! She had learned to be alone, not to depend on anyone. But all of her defenses were crumbling with this man.

Sam turned her and lifted her into his arms, coming to rest on the leather couch against the wall of his home office, holding her tightly on his lap. "I need you, Maddie. So much that it terrifies me. I guess sometimes I'm afraid to need someone so damn much that my whole life depends on it." He released a shaky, masculine sigh as he stroked her hair.

"I need you, too, Sam. So much. I can't stand it when you're cold and remote. It brings back all of my past, all of the times that nobody wanted me." She had already told him the worst. If she couldn't share her emotions, he would never know.

"Fuck!" He raked a hand through his hair in frustration. "Sunshine, sometimes I forget that you have your own insecurities. I was a selfish prick. I was only thinking about protecting myself. Forgive me. Please. I'll try to never do it again. I promise. But I don't think I can stop worrying." He pulled back, shooting her an intense look, his liquid green eyes hot and torrid.

"I want you exactly as you are, minus the frigid stuff," she said, smiling through her tears. She had been selfish, too, letting her fears rule her, forgetting about Sam's past and how vulnerable he had to feel right now.

"What if it's too hot?" he asked, his baritone husky and rough.

She melted and smiled as she met his eyes, his look of desire blatant, his face completely stripped of its icy mask. "Then I'll happily burn," she answered, moving to straddle him, wrapping her arms around his neck.

Sam snaked his hand behind Maddie's head, pulling her head down roughly to meet his hungry mouth. He devoured her, his silken tongue dancing with hers, demanding and rough. She was positioned on top of him, but still, he mastered her. His hands moved to her temples, spearing his hands into her hair, securing her in place for his possession.

She gyrated against his heavily swollen cock as her hands fisted into his hair, needing him, wanting him inside her so desperately that she moaned into his mouth. She was lost; she knew it...and she didn't care. Breathing in the scent of him, tasting him, feeling that massive cock against her core turned her wild, insane to have him inside her. Buttons popped on her button-down short-sleeved shirt and she whimpered against his tongue as his hands frantically sought her bare breasts, opening the front fastening of her bra and cupping her breasts possessively. She panted as she pulled her mouth from his and shrugged out of the torn shirt and bra, letting them fall haphazardly to the floor. "Please, Sam. I need to feel you inside me." Rocking backward, she stood in front of him and yanked at the drawstring waist of her cotton capri pants, shedding them with her panties, standing before him completely naked.

Still dressed in his gray suit and tie, he looked like he was ready to go into a business meeting, until she looked at his face, and his bulging erection. He fucked her with his eyes, his gaze so heated and tortured that she knew he was already anticipating the act...and needing it desperately. He jerked at his belt and unzipped his fly, his hot stare never leaving her body. "Ride me," he grunted demandingly, pulling his engorged cock from his pants.

She looked at his enormous member and then his expensive suit. "It might stain your nice suit," she said hesitantly, but her pussy was creaming at the thought of covering him right now, exactly as he was, rocking his world when he was dressed like a powerful executive.

"Then it will become my favorite goddamn suit. I'll get it cleaned and wear it every day, remembering what it felt like to fuck you in it. Come here. Now," he rumbled, opening his arms to her.

She straddled him and his arms came around her body possessively, his mouth seeking her sensitive nipples before she had even settled on his lap. Her back arched as he bit gently at her nipples with just enough pleasure/pain to drive her insane. Rocking her hips, she slid her clit along his member, moaning at the friction, his cock as hard as steel, allowing her to stimulate herself against him. Hands gliding down her back, Sam cupped her ass, sliding one hand between their bodies from the back, his fingers gliding through her drenched folds.

"Christ! You're so fucking wet. Hot. For me." His voice was strained, his control barely leashed.

"I need you," she whispered, leaning forward to nip the lobe of his ear, feeling his harsh whiskers against her soft skin. His skin abraded hers, adding to the feral wildness that was taking over her body.

Frantically, his fingers invaded her pussy, his breath ragged and hot against her breasts as he stopped laving and nipping at her nipples, inhaling and exhaling as though he was trying to gain control of himself. One hand clutched the cheek of her ass as the other left her saturated folds, and worked to her anus, wetting the star-shaped entrance with her own juices. She gasped as one cream-soaked thumb worked its way into her ass, easing gently into her after breaching her tight external sphincter.

"Ahh…" she groaned, throwing her head back as he eased a little farther into her, gently pumping. It didn't hurt; it was so damn erotic, she almost climaxed.

"Fuck!" Sam jerked his thumb from her, his chest heaving. "I'm sorry. I'm sorry," he chanted in a husky, confused voice.

"What? What is it?" She jerked back to look at his face.

He was sweating, droplets pouring from his forehead and onto his pristine white shirt, his face pale and haunted. "I'm sorry," he repeated again. "I don't do that. I shouldn't have violated you that way." He was breathing hard, his whole body tense.

Oh, shit. Obviously Sam didn't do anal sex…or anal *anything* because of his past experience. Neither did she, but the sense of fullness had been hot, erotic. He'd been so gentle and careful not to hurt her. "Sam, you didn't hurt me. It felt good. It was hot."

"I shouldn't have done it. I shouldn't." He shook his head, perspiration still dripping from his face. "I was just so damned obsessed with being inside you in every way that I forgot."

Grasping his face, she forced his eyes to meet hers. "It was erotic. I loved feeling you inside me. I'm not ready for anal sex, but you nearly made me come. You were gentle. You. Did. Not. Hurt. Me." She stared at him with adoring eyes.

"You actually like it?" he asked, his voice astonished. He searched her face, looking for the truth.

"Yes. You have my permission to invade me any time you want to," she answered, her voice sultry and needy. "Please. I need you." She wanted to take away the remorseful look from his face and replace it with desire again.

"I have to be inside you, Maddie. Now," he rasped, his voice desperate.

She lifted her ass and he grasped his engorged member. They groaned together as his cock slid into her channel. Inching herself down onto him, she clenched his shoulders, her muscles stretching to accept him, panting as he exquisitely filled her to capacity, almost, but not quite, to the border of discomfort.

He fisted his hands at her hips, his jaw clenched, his whole expression feral and covetous. Sam looked beautiful in that moment, his desire and possessiveness so close to the surface, his powerful body tense with carnal desire.

Maddie gasped as he thrust upward, burying himself as deeply inside her as he possibly could. "Yes," she hissed, panting, the air around them humid, heavy, and scented with equal parts desire and need. Her inner muscles clenched around his pulsating cock, her entire body trembling.

His eyes held hers, their gazes locking as he controlled his thrusts, the movement of his cock in and out of her tight cavern.

"I want to go slow. I want to savor this feeling. But you feel so incredible, Sunshine. I can't last," he whispered huskily.

Maddie felt like she was about to incinerate. "Just fuck me, Sam. Please. I love the feel of you inside me. I wish we could stay like this forever." She moaned as he stroked harder, the curve of her ass and upper thighs being caressed by the elegant fabric of his pants with every pump of his hips. Her clit rode his open zipper, the teasing friction sending her reeling. Maddie gave herself over to Sam, completely lost to sensation as she closed her eyes and tipped her head back helplessly.

"Need you, Maddie. I need you," he growled, one of his hands sliding over her ass. "I want to be inside you everywhere. Need to." His thumb slid back into her anus, the area already wet with her juices. He stroked in and out of that tight hole gently while he rocked her channel with pummeling thrusts of his cock.

"Oh God, yes. Yes." Her pussy clenched around his cock, milking him with her spasms. She keened as tremors shook her body.

"Come for me, Maddie," he growled, grasping the back of her neck and pulling her mouth roughly to his, spearing between her lips with his marauding tongue, deeply inside her in every way possible.

Even though she was supposed to be riding him, Sam continued to master her, demanding, insisting, and dominating. The only thing she could do was lower herself down to meet his frantic, deep thrusts…and come.

Ripping her mouth from his, she screamed, her climax tearing through her body like a turbulent storm, leaving her helpless in the aftermath.

"Fuck. Fuck. Fuck," Sam groaned, slamming into her hard as his cock pulsated, releasing himself deeply into her womb, his thumb still stroking gently in and out of her ass unconsciously as he shuddered from his explosive release.

Sam twisted, pulling his hands away from her hips and ass. He collapsed on the couch, keeping her body on top of his by wrapping his arms tightly around her waist. "You're going to kill me," he rasped, belying the harshness of his words by kissing her forehead, her temple, her cheeks, and finally laying a tender kiss on her swollen lips. "I'm sorry. I did it again."

Maddie didn't have to ask him what he meant. "I gave you consent, Sam. You aren't violating me. Please. Nothing we do together is shameful. I enjoyed it. I wanted it. I want you in every way, everywhere."

"I don't have any control with you, Sunshine," he said woefully.

"I know. And I love the way you want me," she whispered, laying her head on his shoulder.

"Do you, Maddie? Does it ever frighten you? 'Cause sometimes it scares the hell out of me," he said, his hand stroking her hair.

"No, Sam. I could never be afraid of you. You might piss me off, but the way you want me makes me so hot that I can't resist you. I want you as much as you want me," she answered him honestly.

He shook his head, his whiskers lightly brushing her forehead. "Not possible, sweetheart," he said, his rough baritone vibrating against her ear.

"So you'd rather have control? Fuck without passion?" she asked curiously.

"Hell no. I didn't say I didn't want it. I just said it can be a little uncomfortable," he answered gruffly.

Maddie traced her finger over the striped pattern on his tie. "We'll get used to it," she mused. "I can't believe I'm laying here stark naked while you look like you're ready to go out and dominate the world."

"You better get used to it. We're getting married," he grumbled. "And I'd much rather stay here and dominate you."

His husky, possessive voice sent a shiver down her spine. "I haven't agreed to marry you because you never bothered to ask. You demanded. And speaking of being demanding, what are we doing about the car?"

"What do you want to do?" he asked in a low, gentle voice. "I want you to have it. It was meant as a gift and I didn't mean to be an ass. It's big, it's sturdy, and it has every safety feature known to man. I'd like you to have it because I worry about you being safe. Nothing can happen to you, Sunshine." He sighed heavily.

Okay…that's better. At least he isn't being a cold, icy jerk.

Maddie sighed softly. "Okay. I'll drive it. See how easy that was? You ask kindly and I respond the way you want me to," she told him with amusement.

"Are you trying to train me, woman?" he snarled playfully.

Maddie laughed lightly before replying. "Is that even possible?"

"Nope. But I don't want to hurt you either," he rasped, his hands continuing to stroke her back and her curls lovingly, possessively.

Lifting her head, she speared him with an amused glare. "So you'll try not to be such a caveman?"

"That's what my mother said," he said, disgruntled.

Maddie lifted a brow. "She said you were a caveman?"

"Yeah. Sort of. But it's not true," he replied indignantly.

"Oh, Sam…it's so true." Maddie laughed so hard she snorted.

"I was nice about the car," he argued.

"After we argued about it," she reminded him, her eyebrows drawing together, daring him to deny it.

"Then how in the hell am I supposed to get you to do what I want you to do?" he asked in a disgruntled voice.

Maddie stirred, sliding off his body reluctantly and standing beside him. "Take me upstairs and convince me," she offered, shooting him her best come-hither look. "You'll find that method much more effective than trying to boss me around like I'm an employee."

He came to his feet quickly, grabbing a throw from the back of the couch and covering her before he swept her off her feet and into his arms. "I have no problem with that system. So anytime I want something, I can just fuck you until you agree?"

Oh, Lord. Maddie shook her head with a smile. Maybe that wasn't such a good plan after all. He could probably get her to agree to just about anything. "Yeah," she said reluctantly, knowing she'd probably regret it.

Sam grinned, a wicked smile that made his handsome face so sexy that her pussy flooded again.

"I want a lot from you, Sunshine. I want everything." His naughty, low voice was sinful and delicious. "I might work on convincing you for a while."

Her heart palpitated as she met his emerald gaze. "I suppose I can bear it." Releasing a beleaguered breath, she smiled.

"I'll have you begging for it." He shot her an arrogant, scorching look.

Truth was, he probably would, and she would love every moment of it. She nipped at his earlobe and then soothed it with her tongue.

"I'll start begging right now if you want me to," she whispered in a *fuck-me* voice beside his ear.

"Goddammit, Maddie. My cock is already hard enough to cut diamonds," he replied hoarsely. "You're a damn tease."

He strode out of the room, and through the house, taking the steps so fast she was bouncing in his arms, laughing as he rocketed to his bedroom. "I'm not a tease if I plan to deliver," she murmured.

"Still a tease," he grunted. He dropped her gently on the bed and started tearing at his clothes. "And you're marrying me. Soon," he demanded, popping the buttons on his shirt as he removed it.

Maddie sighed dreamily as she watched Sam frantically removing his clothes, revealing every bit of his masculine perfection.

Someday he'll actually ask me to marry him.

She already knew she would say yes. If she wasn't sure, she wouldn't be having unprotected sex with him. She had started on birth control, but things were still a little risky, just like the man coming toward her could be a little dangerous.

Gloriously naked, he stalked her by crawling over the bed. He pulled the blanket from her body, uncovering her like he was unwrapping a present, a look of complete fascination on his gorgeous face.

"Give me a date. We're fucking getting married. You're mine," he growled, covering her body with his and pinning her hands over her head.

Maddie melted as his scorching skin met hers, the relief of skin to skin contact making her ignore his comment. His icy behavior hurt her, but her alpha male drove her mad, his dominant behavior making her crazy to have him inside her.

Knowing she would never tame Sam and that she didn't really want to, she met his demanding mouth as it covered hers, losing herself to the man who owned her heart, body and soul...and always had.

Chapter 12

Two nights later, Maddie sat sipping champagne in one of the most elegant ballrooms in the city, trying desperately *not* to look bored. The only thing keeping her mind from going completely numb was watching Sam in his element, charming and urbane, smooth and sexy, and completely hot.

Hiding her smile in an elegant flute glass, she stared at him unabashedly, still trying to accept the fact that he really wanted her, needed her. She had already known that Sam could do a tuxedo with style, but she couldn't help but notice that he was completely comfortable in this elegant setting, a flashy charity function that he'd ask her to attend with him.

In her standard little black cocktail dress and high heels, she was feeling incredibly underdressed, like a fish out of water. She was pretty certain that every woman here had a custom gown with an expensive designer label, and that not one wore costume jewelry.

But Sam was completely sincere when he said I looked absolutely gorgeous. He's the only one who matters.

She sighed as Sam flashed his charming smile at an elderly woman, a flirty and charismatic smile that had the poor woman blushing like a teenager. Yeah, Sam loved women of all ages, and Maddie could tell they were completely enchanted with *him*. Strangely enough, she wasn't jealous. The man she was watching was only a very small part of the man she knew, the face of Hudson Corporation, the public Sam Hudson, elegant billionaire.

But he's so much…more.

Maddie held that information close to her chest, loving the fact that she knew the real Sam Hudson, and he was a scorching hot alpha male with a tender side who melted her heart until she could do nothing but accept that she loved him. Always had. Always would.

For her, there was only Sam. That basic and elemental connection had cemented when they had met, and she had never been able to release the bond. She accepted the fact that Sam was her one and only, that there had only ever been one man for her in this lifetime. Sure, it was frightening, but it was also exhilarating to find him again, to discover that he had been missing her as much as she had missed him all these years.

I just wish I had known the truth earlier. I wish I had known how much he had suffered in his past.

Maddie released a tremulous breath, grateful for second chances. How close she and Sam had come to never being together again! She was a woman of science, but she had to admit that sometimes fate and destiny couldn't be completely denied.

Sam's eyes scanned the room, as though looking for her. Their gazes connected and locked, and he gave her a heated look, a glance that she knew was reserved only for her. Her breath hitched as he stared openly, possessively, his look telling her exactly what he was thinking. The silent communication flowed between them, the heat almost so unbearable that Maddie needed a cold shower.

I was supposed to go to the ladies' room. He wants to know why I'm standing here alone, watching him.

Actually, she had been on her way to the restroom, but she'd stopped to get a drink and then had gotten mesmerized by watching her ultra-hot man lay on the charm with every person around him.

Giving him a small smile, she raised her glass to him and turned to go up the long staircase to the restroom.

"Need an escort?" A low, friendly voice sounded beside her ear.

Maddie stopped on the first step. "Max," she answered, happy to see his smiling face. Unable to stop herself, she hugged him lightly. "It's good to see you."

He hugged her back and offered his arm with a delighted smile and Maddie took it graciously. God, he looked good. There wasn't a single spark of chemistry between them, but there was something about him that tugged at her heart. Aesthetically, she could look at him and appreciate how handsome he was and how well he sported his own black tuxedo. He was such a gorgeous guy, and so incredibly sweet. Still, he didn't appear to have a date. Maybe it was too soon for him.

"Having fun?" Max asked her as he guided her up the stairs.

"Not really," she answered honestly. "I'm not sure how you and Sam do this all the time."

"Do what?" he asked curiously, stopping at the top of the staircase with Maddie on his arm, a quizzical expression on his face.

She released him and stepped back. "This. All of this." She gestured generally around the room. "I guess I'm not exactly a socialite," she said softly. "The only good thing about it is seeing all the handsome men in tuxedos." She winked at him cheekily.

"One in particular," he answered with amusement. "I saw the way you were looking at Sam. I doubt you knew there was another male in the room." More seriously he added, "You look happy. Even if you are a little bored. You get used to it after a while." He shrugged. "It's pretty much an obligation that comes with the money. It's a fair trade."

Maddie shrugged, supposing that what Max said was true. There were certain parts of being a doctor she didn't like either, but she'd gotten used to dealing with it. For Sam, she was willing to do almost anything.

"I'll catch up with you later, Maddie. I need to talk to you about something," Max mentioned casually as they parted.

She gave Max a small wave, heading toward the right to the ladies' room while he went left, probably heading toward the men's facilities.

Maddie quickly used the restroom and paused as she washed her hands, looking at herself in the mirror. She had tried to do a more elegant hairstyle, and her make-up was fine, but she was so…ordinary. And so incredibly different from all of the beautiful women present at this charity event. However, after talking to some of them, she didn't feel terribly inadequate. She was a doctor—she could see plastic surgery from a mile away and some of the women looked downright anorexic. Although Maddie had tried to participate in the conversation, very few of the women could converse about anything other than social activities, fashion, or other mind-numbing topics.

Sam does need me. He needs a woman he can talk to at the end of the day. And he needs love. Desperately.

She dried her hands with a small sigh, knowing Sam had probably always tried to surround himself with people to hide his emptiness. It wouldn't work. She had tried that trick herself, working all the time until she was exhausted, filling every hour of the day with work. But the vacuum had still remained, hidden but present, a void that only Sam had ever filled.

Pushing open the door, she stepped into the hall and walked toward the stairs. She heard the argument as she hit the first step, two angry male voices coming from the hall in the other direction.

"I know you've been calling her. That you took her to dinner. I want you to leave her the fuck alone. She belongs with me. She always has. I need her, dammit." Sam's angry baritone was easy to recognize.

"I want to be her friend," Max argued, his voice firm.

"You want to fuck her. You have a thing for her and I don't blame you. But Maddie is mine. She was always meant to be mine. I can't fucking live without her. So find yourself another woman," Sam growled loudly.

"I don't want to fuck her," Max replied, his voice coming nearer to the stairs, obviously walking away from Sam.

Maddie could see them coming toward her, but they didn't see her. The two men were in a stand-off, shooting each other irritated and downright hostile looks.

"You want her in your bed and it isn't happening," Sam rumbled.

"Oh, for Christ's sake, Sam. Pull your head out of your ass for a minute and listen. I'm not into fucking incest." Max's jaw was clenched, his hands fisted as he added, "Maddie is my sister. My blood relative."

Sam appeared to be rendered speechless, because he didn't reply. He just stared at Max in bewilderment.

Maddie froze, the two men only about ten feet away from her, but they were so engrossed in their conversation that they hadn't noticed her.

Max exhaled deeply and ran his hair through his auburn hair. "We were separated. I was adopted, she wasn't. I didn't even know about her until I saw her at the wedding. She's the image of our real mother. And she and I have the same fucking eyes. After I looked more into my adoption records, I found out she was my sister. I was going to tell her. I just haven't had a chance. I really wanted to tell her first."

Maddie tried to digest the information, her overwhelmed brain struggling to acknowledge the fact that she had a brother. But the notion was so surreal that she wasn't sure how to react.

Joy.

Confusion.

Denial.

She had a brother, and she had never known it, a sibling she had never known existed.

Max Hamilton is my brother. No wonder I feel so connected to him.

She gasped loudly, the noise carrying through the cavernous area. Both men whipped their heads up to look at her. The intensity on their faces made her waver, her heel catching on the luxurious carpet on the stairs.

Reaching toward the banister, she missed, unable to save herself from a fall she knew was coming, her body teetering and unstable. For one very brief instant, she caught Sam's eyes, the fear in his gaze chilling.

Everything happened in slow motion for her, a horrifying moment that she knew she would remember forever. She screamed as she saw Sam leap onto the railing that guarded a very long drop to the bottom floor, his expression determined as he vaulted toward her as she began to tumble, his massive body flying over a treacherous drop that would probably kill him, or at least cause massive injuries. Max's body had been right in front of Sam and her brother hadn't realized she was struggling, so Sam had taken the fastest route to her, the only way to get his body in front of hers. Momentum had them both plummeting down the staircase, but Sam had tucked her into him, his arms around her protectively, shielding her with his own body.

The plummet to the bottom was a nightmare, and Maddie could do nothing but scream into Sam's chest, his arm wrapped around her head, his body taking the damage during the punishing dive to the bottom of the steps as they fell at a frightening pace, rolling over and over until finally, their bodies stopped, Sam's back hitting the wall at the bottom with a force brutal enough to bring them to a halt before he rolled forward, sprawled on top of her.

"Sam! Sam!" Maddie's voice was frantic and terrified as she screamed his name, panicked that he was injured.

He wasn't moving, and his weight lay inert and heavily on her body.

Oh, God. What if he's injured? I don't want to move him. He could have spinal injuries. Please. Please. Let him be okay.

"Maddie! Sam! Are you okay?" Maddie could hear Max's muttered oaths as he crouched next to them.

Max's frightened voice broke through her panic attack. She had to do something. Her whole body was trembling and she was panting like she had just run a marathon as she answered, "I'm okay. I don't know about Sam. He's not moving. I'm scared to move him. I don't know what kind of injuries he has."

She tried to think, to push aside the horrifying memories of him jumping that gulf and protecting her with his own body. He hadn't given a thought to his own safety, his only goal to reach her and save her from injury.

"Oh, God. Sam, talk to me. Please," she whispered, begging him to speak, her whole body tense with the agony of not knowing if he was going to be okay. "I love you. I love you so much. Please be okay. Please."

"Maybe I just like this position too much, sweetheart." His voice was a husky rasp, barely audible, his warm breath caressing her ear, his mouth resting right next to her temple.

Oh, Jesus, he's alive.

Maddie's heart slammed against her chest wall, beating so rapidly she was lightheaded. "Don't move. I'm not sure how badly you're injured," she whispered back.

"Ambulance is on its way," Max said urgently, trying to reassure her.

"He's alive," she answered, her eyes meeting those of her new-ly-discovered brother, eyes so much like her own.

Sam started to stir, groaning as he tried to move off her.

"I said don't move," she demanded sternly.

"God, sweetheart…I do love that bossy, sexy doctor thing you do," he told her, his voice groggy. "I'm squashing you."

"I don't care. Stay," she pleaded. "Wait."

"Will you tell me you love me again?" he asked, levering some of his weight from her with his forearms.

Holding him in place by pulling her arms from her cocoon and wrapping them around his body, she exclaimed, "Yes. I love you. I love you. I love you, Sam. Now stay still until the ambulance comes."

"Sunshine, I'll stay here forever just to hear that," he murmured in her ear. "Marry me?"

If she wasn't so terrified, she would have smiled. Sam was defi-nitely playing this situation to his advantage, but she didn't give a shit. As long as he was okay, she would do anything he wanted, give him anything he asked.

"Yes," she agreed breathlessly. "I always planned to say *yes*."

"Knew you were a tease," he mumbled, disgruntled.

"I plan to deliver," she informed him tenderly, her hand lightly stroking his hair, her relief in hearing him speak overwhelming.

"You damn well better," he grumbled.

In that moment, Maddie knew Sam was back. Tears leaked from her eyes and rolled unchecked down her cheeks as her hands clutched him close, trying to keep him safe until the ambulance arrived.

Max's gaze stayed locked with hers, comforting her silently, his eyes trying to tell her everything would be okay. His hand covered hers, warm and gentle, steadying her as she continued to hold on to Sam. They stayed just like that until the paramedics arrived.

Chapter 13

"Is it true, Max? Are you really my brother?" Maddie questioned Max in a tremulous voice.

Sam had been taken to Radiology to clear him of any spinal injuries, while Max and Maddie waited alone in an exam room in the Emergency Department, sitting side by side, their hands clasped together.

Her hand trembled slightly, the events of the entire evening getting to her. It was so fantastical…yet, even before she asked Max the question, she knew it was true. She felt it in her gut, in her soul. Max Hamilton really was her brother.

Maddie glanced up at him and smiled. Max was right. They did have the same eyes, an unusual hazel that had a sunburst gold pattern around the pupil surrounded by an iris of greenish brown. When she had first met Sam, he had called her Sunshine because of her eyes, saying that the pattern around her pupil reminded him of the sun. Later, he said he called her that because she was the light in his life.

Max squeezed her hand a little tighter. "It's true. I had to be sure before I said anything, but I felt it in my gut. I knew the moment I saw you that you and I were somehow related." Pulling his hand from hers, he dug his wallet from his pocket and sifted through it, extracting an old photo, a small picture resembling an old high school photo. "This is our real mother," he explained, handing the photo to Maddie. "It was her high school graduation picture. You look so much like her."

She took the photo, examining the youthful face and carefree smile. The woman did look like her, with flaming red curls and hazel eyes, her features very similar to her own. "Is she still alive?" she asked curiously. "Have you met her?"

Max ran a frustrated hand through his hair. "No. She died in the late nineteen-eighties, a car accident with husband number three who was drinking and driving."

Maddie had never known the woman. Still, she felt a sense of loss. Maybe she had always hoped that someday her real mother would find her, that the woman who had given birth to her had actually wanted her, but had had to give her up. Admitting to herself that she *had* probably hoped for that rose-tinted scenario, Maddie knew it was the reason she had never really dug much into her records or tried to look for her birth mother. If she didn't know the truth…there was always hope, right? In her youth, the illusion that her mother would look for her eventually had carried Maddie through foster home after foster home, desperately clinging to the hope that her parents had actually wanted her but couldn't keep her, that they had actually loved her. Later, she had simply no longer wanted to know the truth, her heart battered and bruised from too much rejection and hurt.

Fingering the picture, Maddie answered softly, "I don't know much more than the fact that her name was Alice Messling and my father's name was Victor Dunn. Obviously they weren't married and both of them were barely eighteen," she mused, staring at her mother's photo. "Do you know anything else?" Maddie questioned, ready to hear the answers. She had Sam now…and Max. Whatever was in the past wouldn't hurt anymore.

Max took her hand again as he answered, "They weren't married when you were born, but they married before I was born. You were two years old and I was an infant when our father died. He was hit by a car when he was on his way to work one morning, leaving our mother with nothing except two kids and no money, no way to survive." He sighed heavily before continuing, "From the information I could piece together, she had to give us up. I like to think she was thinking about our wellbeing. She went on to marry two more times, probably because it was the only way she could survive."

Turning toward Maddie, a remorseful look on his face, he added, "I didn't know, Maddie. If I had known, I would have moved heaven and earth to find you. I was lucky. I was adopted almost immediately. My parents were already wealthy and I was completely spoiled while you were passed around the system. I'm so fucking sorry." His voice cracked with emotion and regret. "I thought I was alone after my parents died."

Maddie looked into his contrite eyes, her chest aching from unspent tears. "I didn't know either. It's not your fault, Max. I'm just glad you're here now." And she was happy; her heart was overflowing with joy.

She had Sam, she had a brother, and she had friends who cared about her. For a woman who had once felt unwanted, it was everything she had ever needed.

"Me, too, Maddie. I want to get to know you, to be a brother to you. Will you let me?" Max asked hesitantly.

Tears flowed down her cheeks as she looked at her compassionate, caring brother, still looking incredibly handsome even though his tux was somewhat wilted. "Of course. I've always wished I had a sibling," she told him wistfully, releasing his hand and wrapping her arms around his neck, clinging to him as though the bond had already been sealed. From day one, Max had brought out her protective instincts, a need to soothe his pain. It might not happen today or tomorrow, but she was determined to see him happy again in the future.

Maddie sighed as Max's arms came around her, pulling her into a fierce hug. "Finding you was something I never expected, but I'm grateful. I just wish I could have found you earlier. I hate what you went through in your childhood. It couldn't have been easy for you."

She clung to him, tears streaming down her cheeks, already sensing that Max was a man who felt deeply.

Oh, Max. You need to heal. I can feel so much pain inside you.

Maddie could feel Max's loneliness in the desperation of his embrace. Her brother was in pain, but she could do nothing except hold him tightly, hoping her joy in finding him could somehow touch his empty soul.

"Hey...take your grimy paws off my fiancée." Sam's teasing growl sounded from the door. Max and Sam exchanged grins, both of the men looking relieved that they didn't have to brawl anymore.

Maddie released her brother, turning to Sam with a worried frown. "Did the doctor say you could be walking?" she asked, her voice admonishing.

Her heart did a happy dance as she looked at Sam, still in tuxedo pants covered with a hospital gown. He was battered and bruised everywhere, but he had never looked so good. His smile was slightly pained and his normal fierce stride was slower from the pain of his injuries, but damn, he looked good, especially since she had feared he had been badly hurt, or worse.

He gave her a wicked, lopsided grin. "Yes Dr. Demanding, he did. I made him come to Radiology to look at the x-rays immediately. I wasn't staying strapped on the damn uncomfortable board any longer than I had to be." He walked toward her slowly, and gave her a lingering kiss on her cheek.

Maddie's breath hitched, wondering how an innocent kiss could feel so sensual.

Because Sam's every touch is filled with intimacy and it gets to me. Bad.

"So you're throwing your financial power around again, making the medical staff do your bidding?" Maddie asked, trying to keep the amusement out of her voice. She was fairly certain Sam hadn't asked the physician politely. Sam had demanded...and because he was a generous donor to the medical facility, he got whatever he wanted.

"You're a doctor, and it's never worked on you," he muttered, disgruntled.

Maddie folded her arms in front of her, lifting a brow as she met his gaze. "That's because I've been onto you for years. That charming smile doesn't work with me," she informed him, trying to keep a straight face.

Honestly, she could barely refrain from throwing herself into his arms and clinging to him until she convinced herself he was going to be okay. Memories of him vaulting onto that railing and leaping over a treacherous drop to get in front of her to protect her kept haunting her brain over and over like a horrible nightmare. What guy did something like that?

A man who cares about me more than his own life.

"You love me. You know you do," Sam said huskily, a teasing yet vulnerable timbre in his voice, the back of his hand smoothing over her cheek as he said it.

Maddie smiled, unable to help herself. She had heard Simon and Sam banter so many times, heard Sam tell his brother the exact same words. Simon's answer to that particular comment was nearly always…*"Not today."*

She caught his wandering hand and held it over her cheek, her heart racing as she answered softly, "Yeah, as a matter of fact, I do. I love you every moment of every day." Really, how could she reply to him any other way? Sam needed love and she would never again pretend that he wasn't her world. She was done hiding her feelings and not revealing how she felt. He had terrified the hell out of her tonight. Life was too short not to say exactly how she was feeling.

His eyes turned liquid, sparking like the exquisite gemstone color they resembled. "Damn, sweetheart…I like your answer a hell of a lot more than Simon's," he rasped emotionally, his gaze entwining with hers, his eyes speaking volumes. "Do you have any idea how long I've waited to hear those words from you?"

Maddie shook her head, unable to speak.

"Forever," he replied emphatically, his fingers wrapping around hers, his grip almost painfully tight. "Let's go home."

"You haven't been cleared to leave, and you're staying until I consult with the doctor," she demanded. There was no way Sam was leaving until she knew every tiny injury he had.

"Tyrant," he accused with a charming smile. "It's pretty hot. Do you want to play doctor when we get home?"

Maddie shivered; the thought of examining Sam's body in detail would have been arousing if he wasn't beat to hell. Ignoring his sexual innuendo, she answered, "You need to take it easy. You're going to be sore."

Sam frowned and he opened his mouth to argue, but the doctor in charge of the ER entered before he could answer.

Maddie was acquainted with the older, gray-haired doctor, and she stepped closer to him to discuss the treatment and care needed for Sam's injuries. From the corner of her eye, she could see Max helping Sam back into his shirt, leaving his jacket off for comfort. Sam was grumbling, irritated about anything that slowed him down.

The moment the ER doctor left the room, Sam was headed determinedly for the door.

"Whoa…we need to get your script and you need to sign your discharge papers, Sam." She grabbed the back of his shirt gently as he clasped her hand in his and tried to drag her out of the hospital.

"We're leaving," he rasped, tugging on her hand, Max following behind her.

She shot a look back at her brother, his grin lighting up his face as he watched Sam striding hard-headedly toward the door.

Max shrugged and Maddie rolled her eyes. Luckily, the nurse met them at the door, and Sam picked up the pen and scribbled his name on the discharge instructions, barely breaking his stride. Maddie took the papers and snatched the script, smiling at the nurse as she happily followed Sam.

"I don't need the damn pills. All I need is you," he rumbled, heading for the exit, his grip tightening on her hand.

It wasn't exactly romantic or tender, but coming from Sam, the comment was heartfelt and it made Maddie sigh.

Twenty minutes later, they were home.

"Why didn't you take my virginity when we were younger?" Maddie asked as she lay as close as she dared beside Sam in his massive bed. He'd kept trying to bring her closer, but she scuttled away, concerned about causing him pain.

Sam's entire back and legs had bruises forming and he had strained some muscles. Luckily, nothing was broken, but he had to hurt just about everywhere. She could see it in his walk, the pained expression on his face. She had stripped him down to his silk boxers and put him to bed, getting into bed and lying beside him after she had donned a silk nightshirt herself and had practically needed to force-feed him one of his pain pills.

"I couldn't do it," he answered roughly, hesitantly, his hand raking through his hair as though he was frustrated, not quite sure of how to answer.

Maybe at an earlier time, Maddie might have taken his answer as a rejection. But not now. Not after all that had happened between them. She pretty much knew the answer, but she wanted him to tell her. "Why?" she asked softly. "Was it because you were assaulted and molested?" She was tired of dancing around the issue.

"You knew?" he answered quietly, his low voice astonished.

"I read your medical records, Sam. Remember? *Those* records were there, too," she admitted, her hand moving down to take his to reassure him.

"Fuck!" he rasped, his hand squeezing hers tightly, his body tense. "I never meant for you to know. You shouldn't know. I was tarnished. I wasn't worthy of you. I was a street rat who let men use my body." His voice was hoarse and tormented.

"You were molested," Maddie insisted indignantly. "It's nothing to be ashamed of, Sam. It wasn't your fault." She sat up on one elbow, able to see his face in the moonlight, but not his eyes. Sam was lying on his back and his whole body was rigid, unmoving.

"I wasn't molested. I let them do it," he replied flatly.

"To protect Simon," she added. "So they would leave him alone."

"Doesn't matter why. I agreed," he answered stiffly.

"It matters, Sam," she told him softly, her hand coming up to stroke his cheek. "Tell me about it," she pleaded.

How could she tell him that it was even braver of him to sacrifice himself for Simon? He'd submitted to the pain and humiliation to keep his younger brother from being a victim, his father getting payment in drugs and alcohol for the use of his son's body.

Sam released a masculine sigh. "I heard the men talking with my father one night, trying to make a deal. They were a bunch of sick bastards from the organization who got their rocks off by screwing young boys. They wanted Simon because he was young, helpless. My father was going to do it; he was going to let them do that to Simon. Goddammit. How can a man sacrifice his kid like that for any reason?" Sam's chest was heaving as he continued, "Simon was in fucking grade school, still so damn innocent and young. I told my father I'd kill him if he touched Simon and he said he had already agreed and we'd all be in danger if he didn't deliver. So I let the bastard give me over to them instead."

Maddie ran her hand gently up his cheek and through his curls. Her sweet, protective, courageous man had intrepidly offered himself in place of his younger brother. "They hurt you," she whispered, tears coming to her eyes.

"I didn't want you to know, Maddie." His voice was strangled, his torment over talking about it apparent. "You asked me how I got the scars on my back. I got them when it hurt so badly that I fought them. I let them do it, but most of the time they had to beat me into submission."

"My poor Sam. I love you, baby. I hate the pain you suffered and if I could find those men, I would probably kill them. Screw my Hippocratic Oath," she answered harshly. "It wasn't your fault. You were so very heroic and brave. And you *were* molested, raped, and assaulted. It does matter that you submitted to it to save Simon that pain. It makes it even more heartbreaking." Maddie ended on a sob she couldn't suppress.

"Don't cry. Please. It was a long time ago," Sam answered hesitantly, letting go of her hand and putting a muscular arm around her and tugging her along his side.

"Don't. You're in pain," Maddie warned him sternly.

"It will hurt more if you struggle," he answered. "And it hurts worse to not have you close to me."

Maddie's heart melted, and she tried to lay as still as possible against him. "Does Simon know?" she asked tentatively.

"No. Nobody knows except my counselor and now you. My mother would hate herself for it and so would Simon."

"Did the counseling help?"

"Yeah. For most of the problems. I guess I haven't quite gotten over being touched. I usually tried so hard to please a woman that she never really cared whether she touched me back or not," he told her honestly.

"I care. I want to touch you, Sam. I want to please you," Maddie told him in a loving, warm voice. "When we were younger, I was confused. I thought you wanted me, but you wouldn't take me to bed."

"I wanted you," he growled, pulling her close to him. "I was serious when I said I've dreamed about it for years. You were the best thing that ever happened to me, but I felt dirty and soiled, not worthy of having you."

"And now?" she questioned, propping herself up on one arm and running her hand lightly over his ripped chest.

"Now I can't fucking help myself. You had your chance to find a better man. You're stuck with me," he answered, his hand stroking over her curls, massaging her scalp. "You agreed to marry me."

"There is no better man for me, Sam." Maddie ran her finger lightly down his chest, making butterfly patterns on his abdomen with her finger.

"Either stop touching me or you're going to be flat on your back in five seconds," Sam cautioned her in a voice filled with desire.

"Don't you hurt?" she questioned, her light touch stopping at the waistband of his boxers.

"The only thing that really aches is my cock right now. And it isn't from falling down the stairs. Jesus, Maddie. All I have to do is think about you, smell you, feel your touch and I'm ready to be inside you." Sam groaned, his hand coming down to cover hers.

"You're not having sex right now. You're beat up too badly. It won't be pleasant," she told him sternly.

"It will be hell if I don't," he quipped. "I need you too damn badly."

"I want to touch you," she whispered, loosening her hand from his and slipping it under his boxers. "Will you let me? Please. I want you to just lay there and be still. I'll take care of you. Can you do that?"

Maddie held her breath, knowing he would either trust her or he wouldn't. With his past, she knew it wouldn't be easy.

"If you touch me, I doubt I can be still," he warned her with forced amusement, taking his hand away and locking them both behind his head. "But I'll try. I trust you, Sunshine."

She released her breath in an audible sigh, her hand sliding farther into his underwear to connect with his rock hard cock. She smoothed her fingers over the velvet softness of the skin encasing his large member, using her index finger to softly spread a droplet of moisture on the head around the sensitive area.

Maddie felt Sam's body tense, so she kept her touch light, spreading kisses along his temple and whispering into his ear, "You feel so good. So hard. So masculine. I've wanted to touch you for so long."

"Fuck. Maddie," he said in an agonized groan.

"Yes," she breathed softly into his ear.

"Your touch feels so good. So different," Sam choked out harshly. "No pain."

"Never," Maddie agreed. "Only pleasure." She moved lower, grasping the elastic of his boxers and smoothly slid them down to his thighs.

Sam lifted his hips, allowing her to remove them.

"Don't move too much," she reminded him as her hand grasped his cock, moving sensuously along his shaft.

"Right," he heaved, lifting his pelvis for her stroking hand.

Slipping farther down so her face was at his hips, she asked, "Can I taste you? Please?"

There was nothing she wanted more than to taste Sam's essence, but she didn't want to do it without permission. Not until he was used to being touched with love instead of violence and malice.

"Will it feel as fucking good as your fingers?" he asked, his voice graveled.

"Better," she answered with a smile.

"Then for God's sake, take me in your mouth," he demanded.

Maddie relaxed, lowering her mouth to his cock, determined to make this a good experience for Sam. She wasn't exactly experienced, but she was a doctor and knew her anatomy and what would feel good.

She sighed and opened her mouth to finally taste his cock.

Sam shuddered as Maddie took him between her lips, her tongue swirling around the head before immersing his member into the hot, wet cavern of her mouth. The sensation nearly had him coming before she had barely begun.

Maddie. Maddie. All I've ever wanted is for you to claim me forever.

There were no ghosts from his past haunting him. He knew who held him enthralled, whose sweet, soft lips were wrapped around his cock, driving him nearly insane with yearning.

His battered body probably should have been aching, but the only thing he could feel was the exquisite, mind-blowing erotic pleasure of Maddie's tongue stroking along the sensitive tip of his cock, twirling downward and finally taking a long suck like his dick was a lollipop.

Christ! How have I lived without this? How have I survived without her?

Truth was, he had barely existed without her, living every day in survival mode, immersing himself in work and acquiring power, so much control that he would never be vulnerable again. Only to this particular woman had he ever been vulnerable and still was. Did he care? *Oh, hell no.* He fucking needed her, and when he had seen his whole life teetering on that staircase earlier in the evening, he had realized that he would never live through losing her again.

Propping himself up on his elbows, he watched her in the moonlight, her bright hair illuminated as she bobbed up and down on him. Perspiration poured from his face as she licked and sucked, setting his entire body on fire. He shuddered as her pace quickened, her lips tightening around him.

Sam collapsed back against the pillows with a groan, unable to keep himself from spearing his fingers into her hair and guiding her mouth up and down his cock, the erotic sensations bombarding him. He was lost, conflicted between wanting to pull her up and bury himself inside her to claim her or let her go on making him crazy with her mouth.

Mine.

No other woman had ever wanted to please him like this with no motivation other than love.

She loves me. Christ. I'm a lucky son of a bitch.

His cock pulsated and he groaned with abandon as her sweet lips tormented him, up and down, until he was mad with yearning.

So far gone, he never even flinched when her soft hand caressed his balls gently and moved to his ass, her finger gently moving into his anus. She didn't go far, just far enough to send him over the edge, the gentle caress with the tip of her finger so erotic that his head nearly exploded as his warm release flooded her mouth.

"Maddie. Fuck!" he groaned, completely gone. His woman had sucked him dry and he was bucking with his explosive orgasm.

Panting, he yanked her up and over him, desperate for the feel of her warm body plastered against his.

"No. Sam. I don't want to hurt you," she said, resisting. She settled next to him, her hand resting lightly on his forehead, stroking the hair away from his soaked skin.

"Then don't ever leave me. That would kill me," he answered, trying to get air in and out of his lungs.

Somehow, Sam felt like every moment of his life had been leading up to this, to her finally belonging to him.

"Take it easy. Relax. Your ribs were bruised," Maddie answered, her voice concerned.

She had just turned his world upside down, and she expected him to relax? "There hasn't ever been a moment since we met that I didn't want you, Sunshine. Not ever. I wanted you back then, but I didn't feel like I was good enough for you."

She sighed softly. "I loved you then, too. Just the way you were, Sam."

Sam's heart thundered against the wall of his chest and he wondered if he'd ever get used to her saying those words to him. He didn't think so. "Tell me again," he demanded. "Say it."

"I love you, Sam Hudson. I always have," she answered with a smile in her voice.

"We're getting married. Soon." He pulled her tighter against him and grunted with satisfaction as her warm body melted into him. "Don't move."

"I think you're the most stubborn man on the planet," she said indignantly.

"You love me. You know you do," he grunted.

"Yeah. I do," she breathed softly against his shoulder.

Damn. Her answer is so much better than Simon's.

Sam yawned, his eyes fluttering closed. He could feel the tempo of Maddie's breath slowing against his shoulder, knowing she was falling asleep. He lay there for a moment, his eyes closed, savoring the feel of happiness and inner peace, and then he slept.

Chapter 14

S everal days later, Sam entered Maddie's silent house, flipping on the lights as he went, determined to make it back to his house before she arrived home from work. He was cooking a special dinner for her and he had finally found the perfect ring to put on her finger, a heart-shaped diamond surrounded by smaller stones and set in platinum. He had picked it up from the jeweler today, and he was eager to put it on her finger, branding her as his forever.

Looking around her cozy home, he could almost feel the warmth of her personality flowing through the living room, and he was positive he could scent her essence in the air.

This house feels like Maddie.

He wandered the home for a few moments, taking in the mementos and figurines she must have collected through the years, things that would soon find a resting place in his house.

She makes my house feel like a home.

Maddie had stayed with him since his accident, catering to his every need except the most urgent one. He wanted her so badly, needed to bury himself inside her warmth so desperately, that he was restless and edgy. His body was healed. Although he was still black and blue in some places, he didn't hurt anymore. The only thing aching was his cock, and Madeline was the only person who could take care of that particular ailment, one he planned to cure tonight before he went completely insane.

Making his way to her bedroom, he pocketed Maddie's daily planner and some earrings from her jewelry box. There were several personal items that she had wanted before the movers came the next day, and he tracked down every one of them, stopping in a small bedroom that had been made into a makeshift office and library. He grabbed the novel she was currently reading and turned to leave when his attention was caught by a large collection of untitled books on one of the shelves. Curious, he pulled one out and looked at the cover.

Madeline's Journal – 1998

Flipping the cover open, he looked at the writing, knowing it was penned by Maddie's hand. He'd never known Maddie had kept a journal, and it was obviously a habit she had followed for years. There were at least thirty journals on the shelves. The entries were sporadic. Sometimes she went for several months without writing anything, and sometimes something was entered every day. He was about the close the book when one particular entry caught his eye.

I lost my virginity today. Lance and I have been dating for five months and I honestly didn't feel I could deny him anymore. I wish I had. It hurt, and even though it only lasted a few minutes, it seemed like forever. I just lay there and prayed for the whole experience to be over. Lance didn't tell me he loved me. He never has, and I really don't think he actually does. Why am I in this relationship? Am I so desperate to forget Sam, so incredibly lonely that I'm settling for something I really don't want? I feel so damn confused. I hate Sam Hudson, yet as I was hoping for a quick end to my first sexual experience, all I could think about was the fact that it should have been Sam.

Sam's jaw clenched as he read, his fingers tightening on the journal as he read the next entry two weeks later.

I broke it off with Lance. I couldn't take it. Other women think I'm insane because he's handsome, wealthy, and popular on campus, but that doesn't matter to me. All I know is that I can't bear for him to touch me anymore. I have to get totally drunk to even let him have sex with me. It doesn't feel right. It isn't right. Maybe sex is good for other women because most of my classmates rave about it, but it isn't for me. Lance told me I'm not a sexual woman and that I'm cold and frigid. Maybe he's right, but I can't help but think that he just isn't the right guy. Anyway, I'm done with sex. Until I can find a guy who makes me feel the way that Sam used to make me feel, I'm not having sex again. It makes me feel so lonely and hopeless, even worse than actually being alone.

Sam slammed the book closed, unable to read about Maddie's pain and confusion for another moment. It had been so similar to his sexual experiences in the past. When he had sex with a woman, he'd needed to pretend it was Maddie to even get through it. The act brought physical release, but it had also left him so empty inside that sometimes he went without for very long periods of time, unable to stomach being with any woman who wasn't Maddie.

Obviously, she had never tried it again, never found a man she wanted to be with in all the years they were separated.

She abstained and I tried to pretend, leaving both of us miserable in different ways.

Sam put the book back in its place on the shelf and pulled out the previous volume, making himself read the entries from his time together with Maddie. He ran a frustrated hand through his hair as he read, his chest aching as he read about how heartbroken she had been about the incident with Kate. It wasn't as if he hadn't known, but reading her words brought him back to that time and place, made her pain so much more real, and his as well.

That was the day his soul had nearly died. Honestly, he had thought it was gone completely until he had seen Maddie again and she had dug down deep inside him to bring it back to life. The memories had never faded and he'd lived with his actions ever since. Constantly, over and over, torturing himself with thoughts of the pain he had caused Maddie and the agonized expression on her face for years now. Every day he had despised himself, wondering if he had done the right thing, hating himself for breaking her faith in him. His only consolation had been the fact that she was safe, unharmed. But it was a cold comfort in comparison to seeing that broken look on her beautiful face, reliving the experience day after day, and hating himself for being the man who had betrayed her trust.

As he closed that volume, he struggled for breath, letting himself actually feel the loneliness and desolation that had been a part of him for so long. Until he had seen Maddie again. Until she had healed him and brought him back to life. The vulnerability she brought out in him might terrify the hell out of him, but the thought of being without her was a hell of a lot worse than struggling through his fear.

Distractedly, he pulled out the most recent journal, flipping through the pages until he got to the last one, a recent entry that had only been written several days ago.

Sam still hasn't told me that he loves me. I know he must love me because I don't think I could feel the way that I feel if he didn't feel the same. He proves his love in so many ways and I can feel it in his touch. I guess sometimes I just wish he would say it. It would actually be the first time in my entire life that someone said those words to me, and more than anything, I want to hear them first from Sam.

Sam replaced the book on the shelf with more force than necessary. "Fuck! Is it true? Have I never told her?" His fists clenched and his brows drew together, thinking furiously about the past few weeks. He had told her how much he needed her...which he did. But love? Had he really not said those words to her?

"Selfish bastard," he mumbled, chastising himself. She had told him so many times, sometimes with him prompting her, but others when he didn't. Maddie had opened herself to him completely, soothing his soul with her words. And he had never said the words back to her.

His heart sank, realizing that she had never had anyone tell her they loved her. Not once. Ever. Hell, even he had heard it from his mother and occasionally from his brother, and now from the woman who meant more to him than anything or anyone else in the entire world.

"I love you, Madeline," he whispered huskily to the empty room, hoping she could feel it across the distance that separated them.

Sam thought about texting her, but it was something she needed to hear in person. Over and over again. It wasn't that he didn't love her. Maybe the problem was that he loved her so damn much that the words seemed inadequate.

There were packing boxes everywhere, everything in place for the movers to come tomorrow and start packing and moving Maddie's stuff to his place. He pulled a few of them in front of the bookshelves, packing her journals carefully into the boxes and sealing them with a roll of strapping tape.

These are private. Madeline's written emotions.

After he had made sure the boxes were so taped up that it would take a miracle to get them open, he labeled them with a marker as personal books. He didn't want anyone else packing them, possibly looking at them. They were chronicles of her heartbreak, pain, thoughts, and triumphs.

Mine. I love her. She fucking belongs to me. Always has and always will.

As he strode toward the door, he remember Simon's breakdown in their offices when his little brother finally admitted that he loved Kara. Sam shook his head as he locked the door to Maddie's house, finally knowing exactly how his brother had felt at that time. Sam had an irrational fixation with Maddie, a possessive obsession that would more than rival the one Simon had for Kara. He and Simon might be different, but deep down inside, they were much the same when it came to the one woman in their life who could turn them inside out and upside down.

"She makes me happy, crazy, possessive, insane, ecstatic, maniacal…every emotion all at the same time," he said in a perplexed voice, getting into his Bugatti. "How the hell can that be?"

Strangely enough, it really didn't bother him. It made him feel… alive.

Taking a quick glance at his watch as he pulled out of the driveway, his grin broadened. He had time to stop at the jewelers one more time, one more thing he needed to do before he went home.

Tonight, he planned to give Maddie more love than she could handle…in more ways than one.

"He hasn't told you he loves you? That's not exactly a shocker. It took Simon a while. I guess the Hudson men just seem to think we're psychic," Kara's disgusted voice sounded from Maddie's hands-free phone connection in her new SUV. "But you know he does."

Maddie sighed as she made a smooth right turn, bringing her closer to home.

Home. Sam's home. Our home. When my things are moved tomorrow, I'll be permanently together with Sam.

"Are you kidding? The crazy man nearly jumped to his death to save me from getting bruised up and injured. I don't doubt it. Not for a moment," Maddie answered Kara emphatically, speaking louder than she probably needed to because she knew her friend was in another country right now.

"I'm so happy you agreed to marry him," Kara said, her voice sincere. "He loves you, Maddie. I think he always has."

"I know he does." *I just wish he'd say it. Just once.* "How's my future godchild?"

"He's fine. Both of us are eating too much," Kara answered, her laughter and Simon's growl flowing through the speaker in the car. "Simon, I told you it's a boy," Kara's voice was muffled, the last comment directed at her husband, who was probably sitting right beside her. "When are you moving in with Sam?" Kara questioned, her attention back on Maddie.

"I basically already have, but it's official tomorrow. My stuff is being packed and brought by movers."

Kara whistled through the phone line. "He's not wasting any time, is he?"

Maddie rolled her eyes. Sam had called the movers the day after they had tumbled down the stairs, arranging everything in just a phone call. "Nope. But I wasn't exactly protesting," she admitted. She didn't want to be away from Sam anymore. They had been separated long enough.

"I still can't believe Max is your brother. Although now that I know, you two both have the same unusual eyes and I can see the resemblance," Kara mused.

"I still can't believe it myself, but I'm happy. I just wish he wasn't so sad. He must have loved his wife very much," Maddie answered.

"I think he must have, but I really don't know. She died before Simon and I got together," Kara answered thoughtfully.

Trying to lighten the conversation, Maddie asked, "So when are you coming home?"

"Next Thursday. And I still have the weekend off, so we can shop since you aren't allowed to work weekends at the clinic anymore," Kara replied with laughter in her voice.

Maddie smiled. Sam wanted her home on the weekends, and she had agreed. They would both be busy Monday through Friday. Just being at the clinic every single weekday was enough to make her ecstatically happy. There would be a doctor available on Saturdays to see patients who couldn't make it to the clinic during the week, but it wouldn't be her. However, she could review the weekend records and they would all be *her* patients.

She had just finished her last shift at the hospital. Starting Monday, she would finally be back in her clinic.

"Like I really need to shop?" Maddie asked Kara in a disgruntled voice. "There isn't a damn thing Sam hasn't bought me, including this brand new SUV. He needs to stop."

"Um…hate to remind you of this…but aren't you the one who gave me a lecture about the fact that I needed to deal with the fact that I was marrying one of the richest men in the world? I think you even said that I should let him spend his money on me because it makes him feel like he's protecting me," Kara reminded Maddie mischievously.

"Dammit. Yeah. I did say that," Maddie mumbled. She had given Kara that lecture, but it felt so much different when it was Sam giving *her* things.

"I hope we're back before you guys need the jet for your honeymoon. At the rate Sam is moving, you might be married by morning," Kara joked.

"He'd just get another one," Maddie said, bursting into laughter. "He's pretty damn capable of getting anything he wants."

"I take it you wouldn't protest," Kara said with a chuckle.

Turning onto the street where Sam's house was located, she answered, "No. Honestly, I don't think I would." It was the honest truth. She wanted Sam just that much. She'd marry him in a heartbeat.

"Just don't get married without us," Kara warned. "We want to be there."

"I think we can wait," Maddie answered with a smile.

"You better. And we will be shopping for dresses next weekend."

"Okay, okay. We'll go shopping," Maddie told her friend happily as she turned in to Sam's long driveway. "Have fun and take care of my godchild."

"It's been lovely," Kara said with a sigh. "But I miss being home and I miss you."

"I miss you, too," Maddie replied softly.

"See ya Thursday."

"Can you and Simon stop over?" Maddie asked as she brought her vehicle to a halt.

"Are you kidding? We'll be there as soon as we get home. We need to catch up. Later, girlfriend."

"Later," Maddie agreed, disconnecting the call and cutting the engine.

Sam's Bugatti was parked in the driveway, so Maddie knew he was home. Her heart leaped in anticipation, impatient to see his handsome face, bask in the warmth of his presence.

As she stepped out of the SUV, she marveled at how much her life had changed in such a short period of time. Before, she had dreaded going home to her empty house, her vacant personal life. Now, she couldn't get home fast enough, couldn't be with Sam quickly enough to satisfy her need to see him.

I'm not alone anymore.

Maddie knew her life was finally complete.

Bounding up the marbled steps, she unlocked and opened the door, feeling like she was finally home.

Chapter 15

Maddie stepped into the shower with a delighted sigh, letting the decadent jets massage her body everywhere. She was tempted to linger, but her need to see Sam was greater than the pleasure of feeling the hot water relaxing her body. The temptation to go to the kitchen first had been almost irresistible. She could smell something delicious cooking, and she knew he was there. But she hadn't showered at the hospital and needed to remove the stench and germs she accumulated during her long workday before she saw him, so she'd tiptoed through the house to the bathroom.

Quickly washing her unruly hair, she had just started spreading shower gel over her entire body when she felt the hard, unyielding presence of Sam's body pressing against her back. He turned her, letting her back rest against the wall and two muscular arms caged her in, his palms resting against the wall of the enclosure on both sides of her.

Glancing up at him, Maddie's whole body started to quake as her gaze roamed over his fierce expression, his eyes so intense and covetous that her body nearly melted into a puddle of liquid heat at his feet.

He was so big, so hot and so hers.

"I love you, Maddie. I love you so much that sometimes I can hardly breathe." His hoarse voice was raw and emotional, raspy and rough. "I should have said those words years ago. I don't know why I didn't. God knows you deserve better, but you have all of me, every possession I own and everything that I am. I don't know if that's good or bad…but it's the truth. I don't exist without you."

Maddie swallowed hard, her eyes riveted to his. This was Sam, unrefined and unpolished, the core of the man she loved. And he had never been so scorching hot as he was at this very moment, his entire being bared to her.

Tears flowed from Maddie's eyes, mingling with the water from the shower. She lifted a hand and ran her palm over his cheek. "I love you, too. I always have. I never forgot you and I don't think there was a day that I didn't think of you," she admitted honestly.

Hearing Sam say that he loved her nearly made her come undone. Yes, she knew he loved her, but hearing his primitive declaration had her heart fluttering in an unsteady pulse and her breath coming in and out of her lips in ragged puffs.

"I love you, Sunshine. I love you. I swear I'll make up for every time I didn't tell you by telling you so much that you'll get sick of hearing it," he whispered in a husky voice next to her ear as he lowered his head to nip at her earlobe.

Not possible. Maddie knew she could never get tired of hearing Sam tell her how much he loved her. She couldn't regret the fact that she had never had those particular words said to her before, because Sam had been the first to say them, and it was almost surreal.

His mouth covered hers, stealing her breath, mastering her lips, thrusting his tongue between her teeth. Sam's effect on Maddie was to take every bit of rational thought she may have had right from her head.

Steam rose all around them, and pulsating jets of water assaulted their bodies, but Maddie felt nothing but Sam and his relentless assault on her senses. As he plundered her mouth, her arms snaked around his neck, trying to bring him closer. Every emotion she had ever hidden was laid bare as his hands came to hold her head in place for his desperate embrace. Fisting her hands into his wet hair, a strangled sob escaped her lips, vibrating against his mouth.

He pulled back, pulling his lips from hers. "Maddie. What is it? What have I done?" Sam's voice was worried.

"Nothing," she sobbed. "I'm just so very happy. I need you so much."

Resting one arm beside her head and tipping her chin up with the other hand, his eyes clashed with hers, leaving his emotions open to her.

Desire.

Need.

Love.

His expression showed all of that and more.

"I want you to love me and need me, Sunshine. If you didn't, I don't know what I'd do. I'd probably fucking lose it. Need me, Maddie. Please."

His hands moved between them and cupped her breasts, weighing them in his palms, his thumbs flicking her nipples into hard pebbles.

Maddie moaned, her pussy flooding with furious heat, desire to have Sam inside her burning her up. "Sam. Please."

"I interrupted your shower. Now I'll finish it and then I'll finish you," he told her wickedly, filling his hands with gel and moving them both slightly away from the jets so he could stroke the slippery fluid over her skin. His fingers danced and stroked, massaged and teased, gliding over her breasts and circling her nipples until she arched into his palms, begging for more.

He kept her back against the wall and she slapped her palms against it, trying to stay on her feet as she felt his slick fingers slip between her thighs, teasing the saturated folds of her begging pussy.

"Yes. Please." She whimpered as he ran one finger up and down her folds, making her insane to feel him possess her.

"You're so hot, Sunshine. I love those needy sounds you make for me. Only for me. I love the fact that I can make you come when no other man ever has. And no one has, right?" he demanded.

"No. Never." Shit. Maddie's body was on fire, her need for Sam taking complete control. "Fuck me, Sam. Make me come. I need it. I need you."

One hand played at her breasts, moving from one to the other, torturing her with erotic pleasure. His other hand stroked her mound, his fingers slowly delving deeper and deeper into her folds.

"Touch me. Please," Maddie begged, needing him to stop teasing her and stroke her harder, faster.

"I love you, Maddie. I love you," he said harshly as his fingers drove deep, his index and middle finger sinking into her needy channel as his thumb massaged her clit.

"Yes. More. Please." Maddie's hips undulated, begging for him.

His fingers pumped as his thumb increased its friction on her throbbing clit. "Come for me. I want to watch you take your pleasure. Take it," he commanded.

Her whole body quaking, she shattered. Her muscles clenched around his fingers as they filled her, over and over.

Maddie was so lost that she started when Sam lifted her, hands around her ass, and impaled her with his cock.

"Fuck yeah. You're going to come again for me. Around my cock this time," he rasped, his low voice vibrating with need. "Wrap your legs all the way around me."

Maddie had instinctively lifted her legs and put her arms around his neck when he had lifted her, but she wrapped them tighter, loving the slick feel of their flesh sliding together, the gel still not rinsed from her body. "Sam, oh God, you feel so good."

His cock filled her completely, and she shivered from the sensation. Surrounded by heat and steam, their bodies hungry, they both groaned with erotic, feral desire as he began to thrust.

He took her with a combination of primal need and raw possessiveness that had her breathless. Each stroke was a claiming, a branding of her body, and his dominance nearly made her come apart.

"Tell me you need me. Tell me you're mine," he growled as he drove her higher and hotter with every stroke.

"I love you. I'll always need you," she agreed with a whimper, her belly clenching, feeling her climax building to a frightening intensity.

"Fuck. There's nothing better than being inside you. You're mine, Sunshine. You always have been mine," he rumbled, his voice fierce.

Maddie gasped as he pummeled in and out of her with a desperation that nearly bordered on madness, a carnal passion that had her exploding into a climax that tore through her body with so much intensity that she threw back her head and screamed.

Holding her ass with one muscular arm, he kept up his brutal pace, letting her orgasm massage his cock while he fisted one hand in her wet hair and swallowed her scream, spearing his tongue into her mouth, owning her pleasure.

He buried his cock deeply inside her as his own hot release exploded into her womb, and he released his own tortured groan against her lips.

Panting, Maddie lowered her legs to the ground, keeping her arms around Sam's neck to support her trembling lower limbs.

They stood just like that for quite some time, both of them unable to think, unable to speak, their bodies still connected.

Finally, Maddie whispered in a tremulous voice, "That was almost frightening."

Sam cuddled her close to him, lowered his mouth to her ear and whispered back, "No, love. That was absolute perfection." His voice was hoarse and held a touch of awe.

Maddie sighed, knowing she couldn't have expressed it any better than that.

"We're getting married soon," Sam growled as he took a gulp of wine and speared Maddie with a relentless stare.

Maddie was so content she could hardly move. She had just cleaned her plate and was enjoying her wine at the table. Sam had fed her linguini with an awesome Alfredo sauce and shrimp. Really, the man could cook, and there was something really hot about a guy who could master a kitchen.

I think it's hot when he masters me, too. Shit. Sam was just plain…hot.

Maddie stared back at him with a complacent expression. "How soon?"

"Tomorrow," he answered hopefully. "We could fly to Vegas."

"Your mother, Max, Kara, and Simon would never forgive us," Maddie mused, her heart skittering at the thought of belonging to Sam.

"This is about us, Sunshine. Not them. And I've waited long enough. I've wanted you to be mine almost from the first moment I saw you," he answered in a husky voice. "Did I tell you I love you?"

Yeah. About a hundred times since the shower. But I'm not counting. And it makes my heart sing every single time.

"Mmmm…I'm not sure. Maybe you should tell me again," she murmured.

"I could tell you a hundred different ways and show you in so many more, but I got you a constant reminder just in case you forget," he answered hesitantly, pulling a small box from the pocket of his jeans.

Maddie's gaze fixated on the box for a moment before she shook herself and reached for it. Sam moved, crouching in front of her and took her extended hand, opening the box himself. "I've loved you forever, Maddie. Please marry me."

Stunned, Maddie simply stared at the beautiful ring in a bed of black velvet, a piece of jewelry so beautiful and so perfect she was almost afraid to touch it. She had never owned anything so fine, but it wasn't the value of the diamonds, it was the sentiment. The heart-shaped diamond was exquisite, but she knew it had a deeper meaning, one Sam was trying to express with this piece of jewelry.

"You're supposed to say yes now," Sam said in a graveled voice.

"Yes," she replied breathlessly, her eyes lifting to his face, her smile tremulous. She couldn't help the tears that flowed down her cheeks as she stared at the man who had always been her destiny. It was difficult not to believe in fate right at this moment. Two souls that had been meant to be together had somehow managed to find each other again, even though the odds were definitely stacked against them.

Sam took the ring out of the box, dropped the container on the table, and handed her the ring. "I had it engraved."

She took it gently, holding the circle sideways so she could see what it said.

First And Always...I Love You

Choking back a sob, she asked, "How did you know you were the first to say it?"

"I saw your journals today. I read some of the entries. I shouldn't have, but I did," he admitted sheepishly.

Maddie smiled, unable to help herself. She loved his honesty, the way he had come right out and unhesitatingly confessed what he had done. No, he shouldn't have read her journals, but she had nothing to hide from Sam and she never would. "I forgot about them. I've been journaling for years. I probably should have boxed those up myself."

"I did. I didn't want anyone knowing you like that except me," he said jealously as he took her hand and slid the ring onto her finger. "Now tell me you'll marry me tomorrow," he demanded as he stood, pulling her up and into his warm embrace.

"Sam, we can't—"

"Oh yeah. We can." He swung her up into his arms.

Maddie squealed and wrapped her arms around his shoulders. "Sam, what are you—"

"No more talk. It's time to do some convincing," he grumbled.

Maddie stifled a laugh, remembering how she had told him to convince her instead of ordering her.

Relaxing into his big, warm, muscular body, she breathed him in, absorbing the essence that was uniquely Sam.

Somehow...she had a feeling she would end up married by tomorrow if Sam got his way. And as she examined his determined gaze, she knew she would never be able to say no. Honestly…she didn't want to. She and Sam had waited so very long to be together.

As he bounded up the stairs, Maddie almost told him *yes,* but stopped herself before the words left her lips.

Am I crazy? I have the hottest man on the planet taking me to bed to convince me to marry him tomorrow.

Maddie decided to wait and let him do some sensual persuasion. The *yes* was a given, but it could come later…much later.

Epilogue

S am and Maddie were married the next evening, the ceremony private. Their wedding was a joyous union of two souls who had always been meant for each other. Soul mates who had finally found the peace that comes with being side by side, after years of separation, pain and desolation.

Sam had had no problem arranging a jet to fly to Vegas. He'd called Max and his friend had promptly had his readied, no questions asked.

Maddie had made a few token protests, but not very many. Honestly, the ceremony had been a private healing, an experience that had meant so much after the years of pain and separation she and Sam had experienced.

They would have a grand reception later, an event that Kara was already planning as Maddie lay in the arms of her new husband, her mind and spirit rejoicing in her union with Sam.

"I can't believe we're married," she breathed softly, her voice full of wonder and awe.

"You're mine. Forever," Sam growled back, holding her tighter against him as they lay in the enormous bed in their hotel suite. They would fly back to Tampa tomorrow. Sam wanted to take her on a long honeymoon, but they would do that later, after the reception.

Really, all I've ever wanted has already happened. Sam is my husband.

Snuggling against his warm, naked body, Maddie sighed happily. "Thank you for the lovely ceremony. I don't know how you arranged it, but it was wonderful."

They had been married in a private chapel in one of the most beautiful hotels on the Vegas Strip. Sam had been dressed in a tuxedo and she had already had the perfect dress waiting for her when she arrived in the dressing room. Her man had arranged every detail, from the beautiful flowers to the lovely candlelit chapel. The entire experience had been…magical.

"You deserved better," he grumbled. "I just couldn't wait any longer, Sunshine. We've waited so long. I needed you to be mine. I'll make it up to you with the honeymoon."

Maddie smiled against his shoulder. "I thought we just had our honeymoon." Sam had made love to her with such fierce intensity that he had taken her breath away just a few minutes earlier. Her heart was still recovering.

"We're going away together. For several weeks. Right after this reception that Mom and Kara are insisting we have. I want to take you anywhere that you want to go, Maddie. I want to make up for lost time," he said huskily, his hand covering hers and laying their entwined fingers on his chest.

"I'm not sure we have to make up for anything, Sam. Maybe everything worked out the way it needed to be. Everything feels so right now. I'll never take what we have for granted because I know how much it hurts to not be with you." Maddie sighed. "I was focused on school and being a doctor for so many years, and you were busy trying to conquer the world. Maybe it just wasn't the right time for us back then. I'd do it all over again, suffer the same loneliness for years, just to be right where I am right now."

"But I hurt you. And I've hated myself for it since that day," Sam answered, his voice graveled.

"You did what you had to do, Sam. I survived. You need to forgive yourself for it. There really was nothing that needed forgiveness on my part; you were trying to protect me. I would have done exactly the same thing if I needed to protect you, no matter how difficult it may have been," she admitted.

"Would you, Sunshine?"

"Yes," she answered emphatically. "Without a doubt. If you had it to do over again…would you do the same thing?"

Sam was silent for a few moments before replying, "Now? Hell no. I'd strap you to my side and protect you myself. But I didn't have the resources or connections then that I do now. So yeah…I probably would if I was in the same situation that I was then. Your safety comes before anything else."

His answer was so honest, so sincere, that it brought tears to Maddie's eyes. How had she ever been so lucky to have the love of a man like Sam? "I love you so much it scares me," she whispered.

"Don't be scared. Just love me as much and as often as you want. It will never be enough for me," he rumbled, pulling her body on top of his as he spoke.

"No more regrets, Sam. Not for either of us. This is our time. All of the pain of the past has led us to this moment," she told him wistfully.

"Then it's all been fucking worth it because you make me so happy that I'd walk through fire to be with you," he answered gruffly as he caressed her ass and brought her core against his raging erection. "I'll make you happy, Maddie. I swear I will," he pledged earnestly.

Tears spilled from her eyes, his vow spoken like a solemn promise that he would rather die than break. "Oh, Sam…you already have."

A lone teardrop fell, landing softly on his face. "Don't cry, Maddie. Please. I don't ever want to see you cry again," he said, his voice desperate.

"They're happy tears," she informed him as she swiped a hand over her face.

"Don't care. I don't like it," he grunted, stroking his hand soothingly up and down her back. "I'd much rather hear you moaning with pleasure."

Maddie smiled and slid her hands into his hair, sighing as the silky texture caressed her fingers. "I kind of like that myself." Her core heated and flooded with moisture at the thought of him taking her. Again.

He rolled, trapping her beneath him, his large, muscular body covering hers as he told her wickedly, "I could have you making those needy little noises in seconds," he boasted arrogantly.

She bit her lip to keep from laughing, amused by how quickly he could switch from tender lover to alpha cave-dweller. "You could try, I suppose," she told him in a teasing voice.

"I don't try. I do," he growled. "I'll have you begging for it."

Her nipples hardened and her channel clenched, his dominant tone arousing her. "Neanderthal," she accused, her body more than ready for him to make her beg.

"You love me. You know you do," he answered confidently, but with a tiny hint of vulnerability.

"Oh yeah. I definitely do," she responded immediately.

"I love you, too, Sunshine," he answered tenderly, his hand fisting in her hair to bring her mouth down to meet his for a hungry, greedy kiss.

Words were halted as their bodies met in primitive communication, their love consummated in the most elemental, feral, and carnal ways that words couldn't express.

Moments before Maddie completely lost herself to the madness of Sam's fierce need, she acknowledged that sometimes...love really was worth the pain.

It was the last coherent thought she had before she gave herself over to the only man she had ever loved, the man she had waited forever to have and to hold, knowing that Sam had been well worth the wait.

~*The End*~

I hope you enjoyed Sam's story,
Heart Of The Billionaire.
Look for Max's story,
The Billionaire's Salvation,
coming in Summer 2013.

J.S. Scott is a bestselling author of erotic romance. She's an avid reader of all types of books and literature. Writing what she loves to read, J.S. Scott writes both contemporary erotic romance stories and paranormal romance erotics. They almost always feature an Alpha Male and have a happily ever after because she just can't seem to write them any other way!

Please visit me at:
http://www.authorjsscott.com
http://www.facebook.com/authorjsscott

You can write to me at
jsscott_author@hotmail.com

You can also tweet
@AuthorJSScott

FRANKFORT FREE LIBRARY
123 Frankfort St.
Frankfort, NY 13340
(315) 894-9611

9 781939 962324